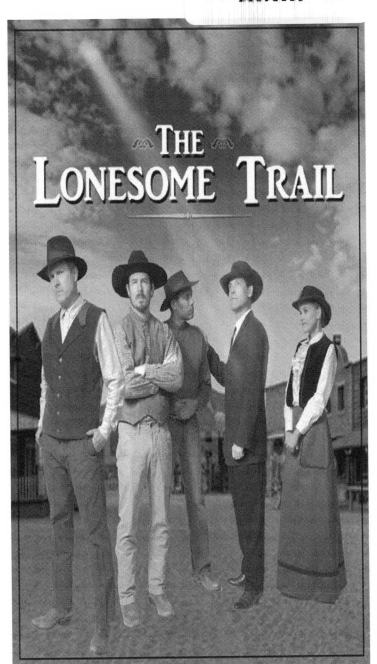

The Lonesome Trail

ISBN: 978-0-9715510-2-2

DEDICATION

I dedicate this book to my mother Inez Rosebud Thomas, who was both a mother and a father to me and my siblings. Thanks to my husband Kenneth and my sons Charles and Joel, without your love and support this would not have been possible.

ACKNOWLEDGEMENTS

In honor of my Lord and Savior Jesus Christ, the joy of my life. God, thank You for all the patience and mercy You have shown me in my life.

Thanks for entrusting me with this book. My life would not be the same without Your forgiveness. In truth, I am a sinner saved by your grace and mercy, not my own actions. Without the breath of your word breathing into my life every day, I would be nothing.

I am grateful to You for showing me that my life motto must be being a doer of the word and not a hearer deceiving myself. I praise God for the Lord Jesus Christ taking the time to show me compassion. God, thank You for teaching me that true forgiveness frees us from the bonds of enslavement that destroy our souls and corrupt our minds. As a Christian, I believe that God will provide the answer through His Word as I always look to Him for guidance.

TABLE OF CONTENTS

Title Page   II

Dedication   III

Acknowledgement   IV

Foreword   VII

Introduction   1-3

Arrival of Preacher Brent Carson   4-16

The Acquaintance   17-21

Settling In   22-34

Under the Watchful Eye of Michael McCray   35-42

A Daydream About the Dreadful Arrival   43-50

Getting New Settlers Moving In   51-60

The Service, The Showdown and The Letdown 61-71

Wedding, Birth, Truth, and Friendship   72-81

The Pain of Prejudice and Ignorance   82-96

Two Different Families   91-103

A Tragedy with Consequences   104-117

The Attack on Homesteaders   **118-134**

Revenge Isn't Sweet   **135-147**

The Prodigal Son   **148-155**

Riotous Living   **156-168**

The Price of Forgiveness   **169-179**

Out of Control   **180-191**

Redemption   **192-202**

FOREWORD

I am humbled to have authored *The Lonesome Trail*. I always wanted to do a western story that would show the spirit of forgiveness in the Old West. The film, *The Lonesome Trail*, is an original story that the Lord imparted to me while I was watching one of my favorite westerns on television. It was a joy to be on the set working on this story and bringing it to life. It was exciting for me to watch the characters come to life in the faces of so many wonderful actors. I started authoring stories at the age of five. I have always loved telling stories.

I have been working on films for more than a decade. During this time, I have authored many stories and produced many short films. *The Lonesome Trail* is my first feature film. It has won eighteen awards and been nominated for 2 awards. This story has been such a joy because of the old western feel of it and how God uses the preacher to do so much to help the homesteaders.

I am honored to share this story and I hope that I will continue to do more western Christian stories. I feel the spirit of Christ rising in this story as the Holy Spirit rises in me every day. I know that forgiveness is extremely important.

As you will see, unforgiveness can destroy a human being when you follow Mike McCray in this story. May God give you a spirit of forgiveness and help you to let go of the past hurts in your life.

INTRODUCTION

After the Civil War, the Homestead Act was enacted to grant free land to adults who did not bear arms against the United States government. Abraham Lincoln signed the Homestead Act, which was an official act of the U.S. government. It was necessary for the landowners to remain on and cultivate the land they claimed. This act allowed immigrants to migrate West and settle on free land with their families.

****

1

In 1890, Mike McCray, was a wealthy landowner in the small western town of Red Springs, Montana. Red Springs was a gorgeous western town, surrounded by mountains that emerged from the endless prairie grasslands and seemed to touch the sky. The smell of coal wafts in the air and drifts through gentle winds from the mines. The heartbeat of the West was evident in everything you saw in this town, from the general store with farmers loading their goods, to the saloon with its loud music and laughter, to the *clink* of horses shoed at the blacksmith's shop.

Mike founded and owned eighty percent of the town and is a powerful force in the territory; he is furious with the settlers. Mr. McCray's face is as strong as iron. It looks like it is worn from the many years of toiling in the prairie sun. His hair is snow white with icy blue eyes and hands like leather. As a settler himself, who founded most of the town, he knows how it feels to work this territory from nothing to a thriving industrious place. New settlers are coming from all over the west into the available land surrounding his ranch. This makes him despise them so much that he calls them "Outlanders."

He does this because he considers them outcasts since they settled on the land on the outskirts of his property. Enraged and infuriated, Mike orders his men to go raid the new settlers.

During this time, the western settlers were looking to move westward to homestead. The cattlemen did not like the settlers changing the landscape of the territory from grazing land to farmland. This caused much tension between settlers and cattlemen. As you go through the pages of this book, the story will unfold as to why forgiveness is so important.

ARRIVAL OF PREACHER
BRENT CARSON

A preacher from up north has been invited by Sister Francis to start a church in Red Springs, marking the beginning of the big change. The preacher agreed and will be arriving on the train very soon. Preacher Brent Carson is a tall handsome clean-shaven man with warm brown eyes and smooth brown hair. He is a barn-storming preacher that calls upon the heavens when he speaks the word of the Lord to his church members.

Elizabeth Turner is a stunning woman, with long blonde hair that glistens in the sun. Her face is soft and wholesome with the innocent look of a newborn child. Her eyes are cold black like onyx stone and her skin is as pink as a rosebud. She teaches the kids of Red Springs at the local schoolhouse. Elizabeth Turner, the schoolmarm, walks to the general store to pick up some new books as towns people travel about the town.

The store stocks flour, grains, and farm equipment as well as beautiful fabric on the back wall for women to make dresses. A barrel filled with apples sits next to a barrel filled with potatoes. When you walk into the store, you're greeted by long wood counter piled high with cookies, candy canes, and sugary sweets.

Several books are displayed on the shelf behind the counter and painted pictures are on the walls, along with bottles of perfume and jars of jam. A table with books by renowned authors flanks the counter, and a beam of light illuminates the dishes on a shelf. Elizabeth explores the books on the table in the general store, trying to find something interesting to read. Her goal is to find the latest Henry James and Oscar Wilde books. A saloon is bustling with men playing cards, while dancehall girls are milling around.

From the window, Elizabeth sees Sister Francis scolding saloon girls and cowboys. Meanwhile, as he stocks shelves, Mr. Jones notices her as she enters. Elizabeth is still looking out the window when Mr. Jones speaks to get her attention which makes her turn around. "Looking for something special, Ms. Elizabeth?"

Elizabeth puts down the books that she has been looking through on the table. "Do you have any new Henry James or Oscar Wilde books?" He walks over to her. "I believe you have seen everything we have of Oscar Wilde. Maybe I have a new Henry James book in the back." Her voice fills with excitement."

Really, Mr. Jones, could you pull them out; I would love to see them." After passing through the curtains, Mr. Jones turns around to search for the books at the back of the store. In the back room, barrels of flour and sacks of supplies are stacked everywhere. A cat lies on a small pile of hay in a corner of the floor. The room is full of crates of supplies, and Mr. Jones starts digging through one of them and pulls out a book by Henry James.

With the Henry James book in his hand, he passes through the curtains again. Sister Francis witnesses a saloon girl in action, Jasmine wearing silky white pantaloons and candy cane striped stockings invite the cowboy inside. Jasmine walks over to a cowboy. Come on honey! The cowboy gets excited and follows her into the saloon. "I need a drink."

Another cowboy sees him going in and hurries to catch up with him. "What about me?" Jenny, the other saloon girl, comes up to him and grabs his arm. "Don't worry, you can come and drink with me." They all walk through the saloon doors. As the door swings open, the sound of people drinking, laughing, and making merry surrounds them.

On the street, Sister Francis cannot believe their behavior. "What a disgrace." While entering the saloon, the two saloon girls look back at her and laugh. Sister Francis turns away in disgust. "Repent for your souls!" She holds a sign that reads, 'Repent the End Is Near' as she walks back and forth in front of the saloon. Sister Francis continues to walk back and forth with her sign, while Mike McCray looks out of the saloon toward the end of town.

Observing Elizabeth from a distance, Mike watches her walk up the street. Long ago, Mike McCray was captivated by an attractive young woman named Elizabeth. Mike often found a way to talk to Elizabeth as she shopped at the general store. Every time he opened his mouth, all that came out were fumbled broken words.

This frustrated and disappointed him so he would often resort to childish behavior. He thought it was funny to pull Elizabeth's packages and pretend to read her books. This was the only way he knew to gain her attention. She thought he was an uneducated, mean, and cruel man and she was extremely afraid of him.

The bartender is cleaning the bar and rearranging glasses. "Mike why are you always looking at that schoolteacher? You are the wealthiest man in town. All the men in Red Springs wish they had your land. Any woman would be delighted to have you." The look on Mike's face changes from proud to puzzled as he thinks about Elizabeth.As the train enters Red Springs, Preacher Brent Carson looks through the train window at the open country of Montana.

The train station is packed with people getting on and off the train with their carpet bags and other belongings. Sister Francis is late; she was supposed to meet him at the train station. He looks around for Sister Francis. A strange character named Carter Dodson approaches the preacher and starts talking to him. "May I help ya, sir? You look a little lost." Preacher Brent glances at Carter, appreciating his help. "I am looking for a Missionary named Francis Barnes.

She was supposed to meet me here. "Excitement creeps on Carter's face because he knows Sister Francis's whereabouts every day, especially at this time. "Oh, Sister Barnes. She's always at the church. She's a "talker that one".

There might be some last-minute things holding her up. Preacher Brent begins to speak. "Oh, well, I guess." Carter cuts him off. "You must be the new preacher she has been talking about." Preacher Brent smiles and reaches out to shake his hand." Yes, Brent Carson is the name." Carter Dodson shakes his hand with a firm grip. "I'm pleased to make your acquaintance."

Preacher Brent prepares to sit back down and wait. "Thank you, sir." Carter pats the preacher on the back. "Red Springs is a great town. Welcome." The preacher sits down on the platform of the train station. "Thank you very much." He reads his Bible while he waits for Sister Francis. He isn't quite sure what to do next until Carter approaches again. "You don't have to wait here. The church ain't that far. You can walk there from here."

Preacher Brent rises and places his Bible in his vest pocket. "Oh, I can. I thank you kindly sir for your help." No bother. Happy to help." A sinister look appears on Carter's face as the preacher walks away. Carter watches the preacher from a distance to find out what his plans are for the town. The streets are bustling with people walking to and from work.

As Preacher Brent walks among the townspeople, Carter appears on the street. Brent spies the church in the distance and begins to head toward it at a rapid pace. Sister Francis Barnes is on her way to the train station, she walks quickly and passes the preacher. Sister Francis turns and realizes she just walked by the preacher.

Immediately, she sprints towards him and stands in front of him. "Oh, my goodness." She shouts "Hello, hello!" Sister Francis attempts to catch her breath. Preacher Brent is startled by her and turns around looking her in the eye. "Yes Ma'am, may I help you?" She watches his reaction and realizes that her behavior was inappropriate. She lowers her head in embarrassment.

"I'm so sorry! It must seem strange to you to have me screaming at you like that. I am Francis Barnes." Her pride is evident as she stands firmly on the ground. Preacher Brent seems comfortable now and reaches out to shake her hand. "Yes, Sister Barnes, I was waiting for you at the train station." Sister Francis shakes his hand eagerly. "I know I was running late; I am so sorry. I was on my way to meet you."

Townspeople are distracted by their conversation and are looking curiously at them as they travel pass. Preacher Brent speaks in an assuring tone. "Well, a gentleman named Carter told me that the church isn't that far. So, I decide to walk, and I am on my way there." Sister Francis motions with her hand to show the way to the church. "Oh, my yes. It's just this way." Elizabeth Turner, the town schoolmarm spots the preacher walking from the train a short distance away.

Mike McCray crosses the street to speak to Elizabeth while she observes the preacher. People continue working in the town, and a general storekeeper is loading goods. As Mike walks towards Elizabeth, he is surrounded by kids playing in the street. She's too distracted by Preacher Brent and Sister Francis.

Elizabeth walks right by Mike and does not see him coming toward her. Mike greets her, "Good day, Ms. Turner." Though she hears Mike, Elizabeth is captivated by Preacher Brent who is so attractive. Mike turns to see the preacher walking up the street and his face changes to disdain.

Elizabeth has a look of serenity on her face that changes to a disturbed look as she sees Mike McCray. Brent feels the warmth of Elizabeth's gaze on him. Brent turns and their eyes meet for an instance and it appears as if time has stopped as they make a connection. Mike moves closer to Elizabeth telling her, "Looks like the town's going to have a new preacher." Elizabeth is captivated by the preacher. "Yes." Elizabeth begins to walk away from Mike.

He takes a step toward her. "Hope he knows we don't cotton to strangers trying to change things?" Elizabeth takes a long look at Mike. "I like to think we would welcome positive change." Mike picks up a stick and begins brushing it across the dirt. "You know I respect your opinion, but we can't just have anybody coming here trying to destroy our way of life."

Elizabeth becomes upset and walks over to Mike. "Our way of life? You mean you and those cattlemen who are so small-minded that they think that nothing should change? You do not look at new ideas or new ways of thinking. The world is changing, and people are changing with it, Mr. McCray." She starts walking away firmly as Mr. McCray follows behind her with a devious smile.

"You know, I always thought your mother shouldn't have let you attend that school up east. You came back a little uppity bookworm of a woman. I thought working at the school would bring about a change in you." She walks up to him and says, "Mr. McCray, how dare you! I am neither uppity nor am I proud sir. I was educated because my father scraped and worked and died in this town for you. Working your ranch and moving your cattle back and forth in the infernal heat of this country."

She drops one of her books and Mike stoops down and picks it up and says, "Your father was a good man. He believed in arduous work and fighting for what we stand for here." She takes her book from his hand and says, "And what is that Mr. McCray, pray tell me? Because my mother had to work washing and scrubbing to save whatever she could to send me to school. After she died, I was left without both of my parents."

He places his boot on the top of a step. "Now that's a shame. I am sorry for that. Ms. Turner, you need to know that I had nothing to do with that." Elizabeth stares at him with a look of annoyance. "Did you help my mother after my father's death?"

Mike tries to calm her by touching her shoulder and she pulls away. "I sent over some things and my condolences when your father died." Her face changes to a very sad and downtrodden look. Her voice lowers and trembles in a hurtful tone as Elizabeth walks closer to him. "She had to work and pay you for that piece of land that you let my father sharecrop from you. You are a greedy selfish man. Michael McCray and I am sorry to say I cannot abide a person like you.

I did not come back to Red Springs because of people like you. I came back here to bring some of what I learned to the people of Red Springs." Elizabeth walks away. Mike chases after her, blocks her, and lightly touches her arm. "Now, it's a shame we can't get along. Ms. Turner, I think you could be a little more civil. You are a lady after all." He smirks as kids run up to him speaking to him. He steps into the street pushing kids out of his way as they are calling his name, "Mr. McCray! Mr. McCray!"

Elizabeth walks away from Mike McCray as he is moving through the children with haste. The kids continue to call out. "Mr. McCray! Mr. McCray! Mr. McCray!" The kids want him to pass out his money and he gives in. The gold coins go up in the air and rain down on the children like gold raindrops.

15

The children scramble to pick up the money off the ground. Some of them pull at Mike's clothes as he pushes them away. "Move now! Move!" He stomps off angrily because the children got in his way while he was trying to catch up with Elizabeth.

THE ACQUAINTANCE

Sister Francis and the Preacher stand in front of the church talking. It is a small white church with a wooden cross at the top of the door. She calls to Elizabeth and she walks over to her. "Sister Elizabeth! Sister Elizabeth, can you come over for a minute?" In the distance, Elizabeth looks at Mr. McCray as he is dealing with the children asking him for money.

Elizabeth briskly walks toward Sister Francis and the preacher. "Yes, Sister Francis, I am coming straight away." A look of adoration appears on her face as she gets closer to the preacher and Sister Francis. The preacher is a handsome man who stands about six feet tall. She notices that he is young and has a kind, gentle face. As Elizabeth comes closer, Sister Francis introduces her to the preacher. "I would like you to meet our new preacher."

The preacher looks at Elizabeth and his eyes smile as he begins to speak. "Brent Carson, so pleased to meet your ma'am." Speechless, Elizabeth replies, "I am so glad to meet you, sir." Preacher Brent appears impressed with her as she appears to be a very charming woman. "The pleasure is all mine, I am sure."

18

Sister Francis notices a spark between them and immediately begins to tell Elizabeth how it was *her* who got the preacher to come to town. "I wrote to the church in Boston and inquired as to whether there was someone available for our town. And what do you know? I got a letter back from Preacher Brent that he would be glad to come and share the good word with the folk here in Red Springs!" Elizabeth looks at him with great interest.

She went to school and was educated and is always interested in learning new things from people who have traveled or lived outside of Red Springs. She smiles, "Coming from Boston, I am sure you find our town to be somewhat passe." He looks down at her stunning face. He sees her small, framed body and sweet and sensitive eyes. He sees her as a respectable woman.

His face lights up as he begins to speak. "I think you have a vibrant lively town here, full of life and vigor." He looks at her with interest and gentleness. Sister Francis seems a little flustered by the chemistry she feels emanating from them both. Sister Francis hurries, turning around, speaking to them. "Well, I have some things to do. And I'm sure the preacher needs to get settled in."

She looks at Sister Elizabeth to signal that it is time for them to leave. "Sister Elizabeth, would you like me to walk you back to the schoolhouse?" Elizabeth appears to be in a daze looking at the preacher and hesitates as she speaks. "Well." —The preacher cuts her off. "You know I would love to walk around and see some of the town before I settle in. I could walk her back if that is okay." Elizabeth beams with excitement, and it is heard in her voice as she quickly responds.

"There isn't much to see, but we do have a lot of good books to read at the general store." Sister Francis is a bit shocked by the impertinence of Elizabeth and starts moving away with her hands on her hips. "Well, I'm sure I don't know. But, if Sister Elizabeth isn't busy, I mean I know she must get along back to the school."

Preacher Brent realizes he may be interfering with Elizabeth's work. "Oh, I wouldn't want to make you late for your class." Elizabeth blurts out instantly her answer to the preacher. "I don't think so; I have a little bit of time before school begins. If we walk briskly, I'm sure you will see a lot of the town on our way. We go right by the school anyway."

Sister Francis has a surprised look on her face. She begins to move away from the preacher and Elizabeth as she takes care of business. Sister Francis is still a little disturbed about the familiarity that Elizabeth and Preacher Brent seem to be displaying. "Well, I do have things to do, so if you don't mind. Preacher Brent, Sister Elizabeth, I best be getting to it." She walks away.

They both wave her away as he puts his arm out for Sister Elizabeth to take hold of to proceed through the town. Preacher Brent and Elizabeth walk through the town as they witness all the townspeople doing the business of the day while the children are playing in the street. Cowboys on horses ride by as the storekeeper loads grain and flour on a wagon. The town is busy, and it appears to be a good place for the preacher to settle in.

SETTLING IN

Over time, the preacher settles in, and the people of the town begin to show up in the church. Preacher Brent gives a sermon and everyone listens attentively. On occasions, the preacher helps new settlers build a home across the road from the McCray farm. With the passing of the years, the Preacher and Sister Elizabeth grow closer.

Today, Brent is walking and helping Elizabeth carry books she purchased from the general store. They are talking and laughing as Mike McCray looks on jealously at them from across the street. Later, in the church, Sister Elizabeth rehearses *Ringing in the Sheaves* with a choir she formed with members of the congregation. Brent leaves the church and singing from the congregation fills the air as he leaves.

Mike McCray is at the saloon doors looking out as usual. As the preacher walks by, Mike yells out. "Preacher Brent! Preacher, I was wondering if I could have a word with you?" The preacher looks back as he walks past the saloon door. "Yes, you can. What's on your mind?" Mike is a hard-looking man who is always armed with his Smith and Wesson pistol.

As a man of his standing, he is well-groomed and wears the best clothes. In an aggressive stance, he opens the saloon doors and walks outside. Mike speaks in a stern voice. "Well, you been here in Red Springs for a little while now." Preacher Brent knows of Mike McCray's power in Red Springs but, he is not afraid of him.

"Yes, I have, and I feel it's getting to be a very fine place." Mike frowns as he speaks to the preacher. "Well, we thought it was a fine place before you came." Preacher Brent studies Mike as he speaks. "I see. Have I done something to offend you Mr. McCray? I'm sensing some tension between us." In a loud voice, Mike steps down from the saloon platform walking closer to the preacher.

"I don't mind you having a church in our town. I think the people here need a good word now and again. But you keep helping them folks move in on my land and that doesn't sit right with me." As the preacher contemplates Mike's anger, he recognizes that he must defend the homesteaders. " I know where the marker is for your land, and no one has moved on to any part of your land.

I have only been helping settlers move on the land across and down from you." Mike walks up quickly on the preacher and gets in his face. "I don't think you understand. I started this town. I am the reason it's bustling and doing well. And it wasn't until the likes of you showed up till we started getting these here outlanders in our territory." Preacher Brent appears insulted by Mike calling the homesteaders outlanders. "Why do you call them outlanders? They are just looking to settle and raise their family."

Mike walks back up to the saloon platform. He appears taller standing on the steps as he looks down on the preacher standing in the street. Cowboys, saloon girls and townspeople are starting to notice the commotion of the disagreement between the preacher and Mike.

Mike continues to speak in anger toward the preacher. "None of them fought and pounded this earth to get it suitable to live on. My family did that. We been raising cattle here for so many years I have lost count. Now you got these foreigners and all kinds of folk coming and farming the land. Raising sheep and all kinds of things that are taking away from water and grazing land for my cattle."

The preacher's face turns red as he gets upset. Preacher Brent knows they are creating a spectacle, but he continues to speak. "Mr. McCray, everyone knows that you started Red Springs, but it's doing fine on its own. With respect to you and your family, no one is trying to do anything to harm your land. But sir, you don't own all the land here and if you don't mind, I prefer not discussing things anymore with you."

Mike is making a spectacle of himself as he continues to rant about how he feels about Preacher Brent and the homesteaders. The saloon is now surrounded by a crowd of people watching their conversation. Mike appears to be fully engaged and furious with Preacher Brent. "You come here with your good looks and fancy words and turning people around. Changing their way of thinking. But I'm telling you that you better watch your step!"

The preacher sees all the townspeople looking on and Preacher Brent looks at Mike with exacerbation and determines he must end the conversation. "Good day to you sir and may the good Lord calm your heart to be a more civil individual."

Preacher Brent walks through the crowd of people, gets on his wagon and begins riding off. Preacher Brent arrives at Sister Elizabeth's house where she is sitting on the porch holding a basket of food. Brent helps Elizabeth onto the wagon, and they drive out to a shady area under a tree. Preacher Brent helps her lay out a blanket as Elizabeth begins to set up food for them to eat. Elizabeth sees that Preacher Brent is in deep thought as he begins pacing back and forth.

Elizabeth's voice breaks the tension as she speaks; he begins to focus on her beautiful face and her golden blonde hair. "I really enjoyed your sermon on Sunday. I really think everything is changing and growing here because of you. I talked to Sister Francis and she said all the families are so excited and happy you came to Red Springs."

Preacher Brent continues walking back and forth with his Bible in his hand. Elizabeth stops putting the food on the blanket as she notices the preacher is still pacing back and forth with his Bible in his hand. "Preacher Brent, is everything ok?" He stops pacing and looks at her again. Preacher Brent realizes that he is not being very hospitable to Elizabeth.

"I have been praying so much Sister Elizabeth. I just don't understand why Mr. McCray is so against the new settlers building down from his land. That is good land, and no one owns it." He throws his hands up in frustration. Elizabeth continues putting things on the blanket and the *clink* of the plates pierce the air. Elizabeth looks up at Preacher Brent and speaks in a firm tone.

"Mike McCray thinks he owns everything and everyone in Red Springs. He thinks his family is the reason for the town doing so well. And he thinks just because they started everything that means that no one else can do anything in this town." The preacher, seeming to calm down, begins to sit down. He leans back and relaxes with his legs crossed on the blanket.

"I just want to help him understand what we are doing is building a great place here. We have so many wonderful people moving into our town. They just want to build and bring good families in to settle down and raise their children." Elizabeth is still stirred up and has a stern look on her face. "You will never get through to him. He is pigheaded and prideful." Preacher Brent looks over at Elizabeth and speaks in a humble voice.

"We are all God's people, Sister Elizabeth. I just think we need to pray for him more and ask the Lord for guidance." Elizabeth lowers her head in shame realizing she has displeased the preacher. "I'm sorry, I have known his family my whole life and they have all been like that. But you are right, I should pray for them." Elizabeth places their lunch out, a beautiful spread of sandwiches, rolls, chicken, corn, and beans. A big jar of Lemonade sits in the middle with beads of water slithering silently down the glass.

Preacher Brent realizes Elizabeth has gone through a lot of trouble to make a pleasant day for them. Preacher Brent sighs guiltily, "I am so sorry; I should be enjoying this good food you have made. I don't know why you even spend time with me. I am so obsessed with helping everyone. I sincerely love God's people."

Elizabeth touches his hand in reassurance, a small gesture of her faith in him. "That's what I like about you. I never met a man that can hold his temper like you. I mean who sincerely stands by what he believes. I truly admire your kind and generous heart." Preacher Brent looks at her with tenderness and realizes that she is a true match for his heart.

29

Preacher Brent lowered his voice softly. "I don't know about a kind and generous heart. It took everything in me to walk away from McCray today." Brent jerks his fist into the air as he stands to his feet with a frustrated look on his face. "I felt like knocking him flat on his back. That's not in God's word." Elizabeth sees his Bible on the blanket and reaches over and touches it. She looks over at him with a look of adoration.

"The Good Book says we should turn the other cheek, but it doesn't say it will always be easy to do so." She smiles at him. "You're a man too, Brent Carson." He realizes now is the time to ask her to marry him. "I am a man and as a man, I think it's about time we started talking about." —— He is interrupted as he spies some people riding up. It appears to be a Mexican family. Elizabeth looks up and sees a family coming across the field in the distance. "Well, I wonder who they are?"

It is the Gomez family who have traveled through the western prairie to reach Red Springs. Mr. Francisco Gomez looks worn from their travels. He is a dark-haired man with a sombrero on his head to keep the sun off his neck but failed to keep the dust off his clothes.

He pulls one horse that is dragging their possessions, with his daughters Rosita and Inez riding on it, and his wife Angelica walking beside him. They are beautiful little girls with long shiny black hair. Angelica is a handsome woman who is wearing a flowered dress with a shawl thrown around her neck. Elizabeth and the preacher are seated when Francisco Gomez walks up to them.

After getting up, the preacher walks over to meet the Gomez family. "Hi, looks like you folk can use some help." Angelica looks up at him and sees he has a friendly face. "Yes, we are looking for Red Springs." Francisco Gomez walks over and introduces himself. "I'm Francisco Gomez and this is my wife Angelica." Francisco motions to her and touches her hand.

Elizabeth looks at the beautiful little girls on the horse. Angelica notices her looking at her daughters and quickly introduces them to Elizabeth. "I am so sorry, where are my manners.? Yes, I'm Angelica and these are our little ones, Inez and Rosita." Inez is a little tall for her age and very skinny, yet her hair comes all the way down her back. Her eyes are coal black.

Inez has a very lovely face. As she looks at the preacher, Inez has a warm look in her eyes. Rosita is very small with an attractive face. Rosita rubs the horse, soothing it, as she looks at it with joy in her eyes. Seeing the children's sweet faces, the preacher walks over to them. "Well, aren't they the sweetest little ones? Well, this is Red Springs.

What brought you folks to our town?" Francisco wears a proud expression on his face as he watches his family being adored by such kind people as Preacher Brent and Elizabeth. As he ties his horse to a nearby tree, he takes his two girls from the horse. "We want to settle on some nice land and raise our little ones." The picturesque prairie looks like a soft green blanket as he gazes out.

As he hears the birds above, Francisco looks at Preacher and takes a deep breath as he takes everything in. "We don't have much. But we hope to grow some crops and make us a little money selling them and live off the rest." Elizabeth looks at Angelica and sees she must be worn from the long trip. "Well, you must be so tired. You look like you been traveling for days."

The preacher puts his hand on Francisco's shoulder assuring him that he is welcome. Well, let's see if we can help you. Maybe we can move them over near Barnaby and his family. An expression of delight appears on Elizabeth's face. "Yes, that is a great idea. Barnaby is such a wonderful man. He is our local healer. He has birthed all the children of the settlers. Anything you have ailing you, he has an herb for it."

Angelica looks at Francisco and grabs his hand as she is overcome with emotion. "You folks are a godsend. I can't believe we are finally going to make a home for good." Angelica wipes a tear from her face. Francisco looks over at his wife and holds her hand. "You folks have to excuse Angelica because she's been toting things around for a long time. We fell on hard times and just weren't able to get things started."

Preacher Brent puts his hand on Francisco's shoulder again to console him. "You know God always has a way for his people. Now, don't you fret? We are going to do our best to help you get settled in right, Sister Elizabeth?" Elizabeth looks at him and smiles. "Yes, we are."

Elizabeth notices Rosita looking at the food that is spread out on the blanket. Elizabeth says, "What am I thinking? You must be hungry after your long trip." Francisco and Angelica look at each other and breathe a sigh of relief. Preacher Brent walks over and sits down on the blanket to prepare to eat. "Well, I'm hungry. And there's plenty here if you are inclined to join us."

Angelica walks over to the blanket and sees all the delicious looking food. " If you don't mind. I guess we could share in your meal. I know the children are hungry." Rosita and Inez walk over and sit down on the blanket. Elizabeth begins passing food to the children. Elizabeth says, "Okay! Well, here are some biscuits for you."

Elizabeth gives some plates to Angelica, and she hands one to Francisco. "Here, have some lemonade. What else do I have here?" She looks in her basket, which contains a variety of goodies. Everyone is having a great time sitting, laughing, and talking.

UNDER THE WATCHFUL EYE OF
MICHAEL MCCRAY

everal minutes later, Preacher Brent, Elizabeth, and the Gomez family have packed up their belongings and are loading them into a wagon. Preacher Brent and Francisco help Rosita, Inez, Elizabeth, and Angelia on after Francisco ties the horse to the wagon. Preacher Brent pulls back on the reigns of his horse leading them away. A beautiful green pasture leads them to Bill Barnaby's farm. The soft wind rolls across the long grass like waves.

After arriving at the Barnaby farm, everyone goes to meet Bill Barnaby and his family. Mike McCray lurks in the background afar off through a steeply forested part of Barnaby's land. There is a rhythmic sound of cows grunting and humming in the distance as cowhands ride horses to wrangle up the cattle. Mike McCray is unmoved as he is focused on Preacher Brent, Elizabeth, Francisco, Angelica, and the children as they are walking around near his land.

After a long time of watching, Mike rides off. Preacher Brent brings the Gomez family to meet Bill, Matt, and Alice Barnaby. Bill is busy planting some crops in the ground and tilling and tossing rocks that he finds to the side.

As they walk up, Alice and Matt help Bill with the clearing of rocks and planting in the field. Preacher Brent walks over to Bill. "Hey, Bill, I have some folk here I want you to meet!" Bill stops plowing and wipes his hands on his pants. "Hey, preacher. How you folks doing? Welcome. Ms. Elizabeth." Elizabeth seems to have a bright light shining from within as she smiles with enthusiasm for the new settlers.

Bill, we just met these nice folks out in the open range traveling toward Red Springs. As Bill wipes his hands again with a cloth, he walks up to Preacher Brent to shake hands and meet the new settlers. Preacher Brent speaks with pride as he introduces the Gomez family. "Yes, we broke bread with them and been talking to them for a few hours. Feel like we have known them for a mighty long time too."

Alice and Matt are working on some planting, and they put their tools down as they notice the new settlers going over to greet them. Francisco puts his hand out to shake Bill's hand with enthusiasm. "It is sure nice to meet you folks. The preacher and Sister Elizabeth said you wouldn't mind us moving onto this land right next to you."

Bill looks at the preacher with concern but tries to mask it for the new settlers. Bill puts on a smile. "No, that's not a problem at all. Ms. Elizabeth, why don't you show the folks the land over there and I can chat a spell with the preacher." Elizabeth motions to Alice and the Gomez family to follow her. "That's a wonderful idea. Let's get you folks things. She starts taking them straight down a wooded path near Bill Barnaby's land.

Elizabeth and Alice walk off with Francisco and Angelica and the children to a beautiful grassy area of land that has lovely oak trees in the distance. Angelica becomes overwhelmed as she sees such a stunning piece of land that she will be settling on. "Oh, Francisco it is so delightful. I think we have found our new home." He walks over and hugs his wife. Francisco looks at Angelica and says, "Yes, I believe we have too. Thank God for his goodness."

Inez notices that her mother is overcome with emotion. "Pa, I think mom's crying." Angelica tries to cover up her crying by getting the children settled. "No I ain't, I just got something in my eye is all. I'm fine. Well, come on now, you children need to start getting your belongings together. Let's get our stuff and set up camp."

Francisco looks at Elizabeth with gratitude as he realizes that he is experiencing a true blessing. Sister Elizabeth, "Stuff like this don't just happen. I mean, we been around, and people aren't always as nice as you folk. I don't know how to thank you." Elizabeth sees Francisco is appreciative of all the help they gave his family. "Don't you worry about it. Preacher Brent helps a lot of people in Red Springs; he is a true man of God.

He truly believes in helping thy neighbor. He's a good man." Francisco takes his hat off and wrings it in his hands looking down at the ground a moment and quickly hugs Angelica tight. After the Gomez family leaves, Preacher Brent notices Bill Barnaby is still plowing the land and the preacher approaches him to get his attention while he is working the land. Bill stops plowing and turns around speaking to him in an irritated tone.

"Preacher, now you listen to me. I know you love helping folk and all, but you know that land is too close to McCray's land." Preacher Brent's face changes to a concerned look. Bill continues to talk. "You remember what happened when you moved us over here. He wasn't none too happy about it."

Preacher Brent looks out at all the land around him. "Bill, you know this is free land. Anybody who wants to lay claim can." Bill walks over toward the barn. Bill walks back and forth and starts lifting hay bales and putting them in the barn. Bill throws his pitchfork in the hay. "I know you believe that everyone has some good in them. McCray owns this territory, and sooner or later something is going to happen. You keep putting dynamite on a lit fire."

Preacher Brent walks up close to Bill and looks at him for a moment. Bill calm down. Bill starts tossing the hay bales again. "This is serious, preacher!" The Preacher piers up at the clouds above and starts moving his hands and he speaks. "God intended for me to help people and these people came around when Sister Elizabeth and I were having an outing. They just happened by. They had been trying to find Red Springs anyhow.

Was I supposed to turn them away with the little children and everything? They looked like they hadn't eaten nothing in a while." The preacher sits on the edge of the barn looking out at the land. There is scenic green grass and crops as far as the eye can see and fruit trees line the land far off on McCray's farm.

In the distance, McCray's ranch shows through the trees as the land is filling up with homesteaders. Preacher Brent sees the families who are working their land. "My calling is to help God's people. I can't turn my back on a single soul." Bill starts pacing as he is very upset and uncomfortable with the preacher moving more people on the land. "Don't you remember what happened when my family and I came here?" He hops down from the barn.

Preacher Brent walks over closer to Bill. "Bill. I do, but things are different now." Bill moves back from him and grabs a hoe and starts working his land again. His voice raises as he is now extremely upset. "Different! What world are you living in? This is 1887. Many a Negro have been lynched by white folks for just being alive. These people respect you, the town's people, and everyone.

If Mr. McCray wasn't afraid of Ms. Elizabeth hating him all together for harming you, he would have gone against you long ago. That man got a lot of power round these parts." The preacher looks troubled as he walks over to Bill. He touches him on the shoulder to calm him.

"What's wrong Bill? You had anymore run-ins with the McCray's or their men?" Bill climbs up on the edge of the barn and sits.

THE DREADFUL ARRIVAL

Bill appears distraught. He removes his hat and starts wringing it in his hands. "No. But I still remember that night like it was yesterday." Bill begins to think about what happened to him when he came to Red Springs. He is in deep thought and the preacher notices that he seems to be daydreaming. He is thinking about three years earlier when his family was passing through the town in a wagon with his wife, Alice Barnaby and son, Matt Barnaby.

In a fit of rage, Mike McCray runs out of the saloon and walks up to the wagon in a huff after seeing the wagon from the saloon window. Mike's men come running out of the saloon and surround the wagon in a threatening manner. Mike hurries up to the wagon right next to Bill. " You lost boy?" He startles Bill Barnaby into silence and Bill and Alice have a look of terror on their faces as

Bill looks over at Mike. Mike moves closer to the wagon and looks at Bill with fervor and says, "What's wrong with you? Didn't you hear me ask you a question?" In the distance, Preacher Brent is walking up the street from the church and sees that there may be trouble. He begins walking faster to hurry to get to the wagon.

He arrives and see's Mike McCray and all his men surrounding Bill Barnaby and his family. Preacher Brent asks, "Is everything okay here?" Mike looks at the preacher with anger in his eyes. "This ain't got nothing to do with you. I'm talking to him." He says, "What's your name boy?" With the look of distress on his face, Bill says, "Bill ah Bill sir. Bill Barnaby." Preacher Brent walks over to him and touches the side of the wagon nearest to Bill.

Preacher Brent looks up at Bill and catches his eye. "This here is one of our new settlers." Bill looks at him surprised and says, "What!" Bill quickly changes the look as he realizes the preacher is trying to save his life. "I mean. yes sir." Preacher Brent looks at Bill assuring him that he will be fine.

Mike responds in an agitated tone. "Is that true boy? You coming to settle here out there with the preacher and all them folk?" Alice looks at Bill with great fear as she peers through the curtain cover of the wagon to see Matt asleep inside. She grabs Bill's hand, squeezes it tight and Bill feels Alice's fear and knows he must remain calm. "Yes sir. my family and I been travelling and looking for this here preacher."

The crowd of men start to talk among themselves and the anger and rage of the men travel through the air. Their voices are heard by Bill and Alice and they can feel that the men want to harm them. Mike looks at his men and puts his hand up to signal for them to calm down as he turns to Preacher Brent and moves closer.

He says, "I don't know if I like that, preacher. You are bringing all kinds of people to settle here. I think this time, you've gone too far!" Elizabeth is walking up from the church with Sister Francis Barnes from a meeting at the church. She sees a crowd of townspeople have formed across the street from the saloon with Preacher Brent and Mike McCray where there appear to be some angry men surrounding a wagon with a negro family.

Sister Francis looks over and notices all the commotion. "Oh, my goodness! What shall we do?" Elizabeth picks up her pace, walking faster toward them. Pray for God to help us. That's all we can do. Sister Francis looks concerned. "But the preacher, he might get hurt." Elizabeth looks over at Sister Francis with comforting eyes as she walks away. "Preacher Brent knows what he's doing."

Sister Francis turns and responds in a shocked tone. "But for a "darkee"?" Elizabeth stops and looks at her with a shocked look on her face. "Sister Francis, how dare you! We are all God's children." Sister Francis bows her head in shame and looks up at Elizabeth as she is walking off and says, "I'm sorry, you're right. If Preacher Brent welcomes them, then we will all accept them too."

As Elizabeth races across the street, she attempts to push through the crowd to get to Mike and get in his face. "Mr. McCray, what is the meaning of this? What are your men coming against this man and his family for?" People in the crowd are now talking among themselves and the noise is becoming louder. The atmosphere is filled with tension and Alice and Bill are both frightened.

Preacher Brent looks at Alice and Bill with a calming expression on his face while turning away from the crowd. Preacher Brent then turns and touches Elizabeth's shoulder to let her know everything is under control. "Sister Elizabeth, everything is under control." He moves closer to Mike and says, "Isn't it, Mr. McCray?"

Mike looks at him and looks into Elizabeth's angry eyes. "Yes, it's under control." He turns to the crowd and his men and says, "Why are all you people standing here? Go home to your families!" The men disband, looking around at Bill and his family. The townspeople start to leave and head back toward the town. The preacher asks Bill, "Is it okay to come aboard? Bill says, "I reckon."

The preacher says, "I just want to get you and your family out of harm's way." Preacher Brent begins to climb into the wagon. Bill turns and begins to thank him for his help. "I don't know how we can even begin to thank you folks for what you did for us." Preacher Brent touches Bill's hand, urging him to start driving out of town. I suggest you hush and let's move down the road a bit.

Mike McCray and some of the men are still looking on from across the street in front of the saloon. Sister Francis lets them know she is going home. I think I will be heading home too. Preacher Brent tries to assist Sister Francis with a ride. "I think we can fit you ladies on board. Let me help you." Elizabeth climbs into the wagon. "Thank you." Sister Francis has a strange look on her face.

48

The preacher reaches out to help her onto the wagon. " I don't think so, preacher." The preacher looks at Elizabeth. They ride out of town. Bill and Alice are more comfortable as they are heading through the countryside. Bill looks at the preacher and asks a question about the people in the town. "You got a lot of folk like us around here?" Bill responds to Preacher Brent with a hint of humor and sarcasm, as Alice looks at him with a confused expression on her face.

Elizabeth sees the look on Alice's face and reaches out and grabs Alice's hand. "Don't you worry, Preacher Brent helps a lot of people settle in and homestead here in Red Springs." As the sound of the horses trotting fills the air, they ride onto the open country. Bill turns to the preacher to let him know that they don't plan to settle in Red Springs. "About that. We were just passing through. I do some doctoring for my people here and there." Preacher Brent gets an excited look on his face.

"You a doctor? Oh, we need a doctor." Bill tries to let the preacher know he is not an educated doctor. "No. I didn't say I was a doctor who had been schooled and learned. I said I done helped with herbs and things, birthing, and babies and all."Preacher Brent is so excited to hear that Bill can deliver babies.

He ignores everything else Bill said. "Birthing babies! We got a family here and the doctor in town is too expensive. It sure would mean a lot if you could help them. When their time comes, I mean." Startled by what the preacher just said, Elizabeth touches the preacher to get his attention. "Preacher, I think you should talk to the family first. I mean." Elizabeth appears to be uncomfortable and worried. Preacher Brent is happy that Bill will be doctoring families.

"Nonsense! They don't have money to pay right now. And Bill is going to help us out." The sound of the wagon wheels on the ground rings out in the air as the sun is going down as they ride on the prairie toward the homestead land. Bill pierces the silence. "Right." Then Bill looks at Preacher Brent and said, "Yes, sir, but I never said I did it for free." Then Bill clicks with his mouth to signal the horses to move a little quicker.

GETTING NEW SETTLERS MOVED IN

Bill sits on the edge of the barn. The sound of birds rings out overhead. Preacher Brent walks over to Bill who seems to be frozen in thought and says, "Are you okay?" Bill is a little startled from his daydream and says, "Huh. I was just in deep thought." Preacher Brent says, "I know a lot happened to you when your family first came here. It has been a long time now."

Having woken up from his daydream, Bill recalls the events of that terrible day. He climbs down from the barn ledge and begins putting hay into a pile with a pitchfork. The noise of horses pierces the air in the barn nearby as Matt Barnaby is brushing down the horses and overhears Bill and Preacher Brent's conversation. Preacher Brent shoos some chickens away as he walks over to Bill.

Preacher Brent says, "Everything worked out just fine, didn't it?" A frustrated Bill throws some more hay and picks it up rapidly as he is talking with Preacher Brent. Bill says, "Just fine! They were about to hang me, kill me and my whole family. That is something I've heard about. In my travels, I've seen men hanged. I have avoided it most of my life by keeping on the move.

But that night, was when I realized God could use a crazy white preacher and his woman to save me." Matt sets down the brushes and rubs the horse as he begins walking out of the stall and closes the door. As he walks over to Preacher Brent and Bill , Matt wipes his hands on his shirt. "Hey, Preacher Brent, I see you done brought a new family to settle here." Preacher Brent smiles with pride. "Yeah, Sister Elizabeth and I met them out in the open range earlier today! They were heading to Red Springs to settle down."

Matt looks at all the many homesteaders all around and sees some of them working on a new abode in the distance. "Wow! Seems we are going to be running out of land soon to put folk." Brent looks around and sees a family tending to crop in a field. "I guess you might be right Matt. But, if we can bring them in, we will."

Matt walks up and grabs a hoe and starts chopping through the hard dirt. "Well, let me get on back to my chores for I get too behind." Bill stands tall as he watches his son working on their land. "Yeah, son, I'll be over there to help you with some of that plowing in a minute. Just finishing up with the preacher here."

Matt nods his head and pulls his hat down a little to block out the glare of the sun from his eyes and continues to beat the ground with his hoe. "Ok. It looked like you were pretty involved in your story. " Bill goes into the barn and begins picking up the bridles and wiping them off as the preacher follows him. Bill is busying himself with chores while he speaks to the preacher. "See, even my boy notices we getting to our limit.

You can't admit it just like you can't admit how much of a horror that night we came here could have been."Preacher Brent begins to look down at the ground and he looks up at Bill. "Okay. Okay, I'll admit it was a little hairy. I know. I know I'm not like other white men. I get that." Bill is still frustrated and responds in a sarcastic tone. "Really, you don't say."

Preacher Brent speaks to him in an aggravated tone. "But Bill, I done told you a hundred times I don't believe in hating anyone no matter what color." Bill grabs a cloth from the shelf and wipes his hands. "That's good I respect that, but Preacher..." Preacher Brent interrupts Bill, takes a breath and blurts out what he feels with a strong tone.

"Let me finish. My family was dirt poor. We were considered outcasts just because we didn't have money, breeding or education enough to fit into Boston society. You don't fit in without money and breeding." Bill turns to him and shouts. "But you ain't a Negro! You're a white man. I ain't never lived under no white man's protection." Preacher Brent puts his hand on Bill's arm to get his attention.

"You're living under God's protection, not mine." Bill's eyes change as he seems to calm down a little. "You're right, I do believe that." Then Bill raises his voice to make another point. "Or I would not have stayed! I would have got out of here as fast as I could that night!" Preacher Brent looks at him with appreciation while he touches Bill's shoulder to calm him. " I'm glad you stayed."

Bill turns around with a reverent look on his face. "I know you're a man of the church and I am just a man. But the good Lord knows how much one man can do. And I think you done did all you can to help people."Preacher Brent is distracted for a moment by the noise of some geese flying overhead. "That's for the good Lord to determine."

55

Bill motions to the land before them and Bill and Preacher Brent look out and see all the trees and log cabins that the homesteaders have built. In the distance, Bill sees they are getting closer to McCray's land. "I mean it! You got to start turning them away because soon, you will be moving too close to McCray land. And I think this might be that time." The preacher looks up at the sky with devotion to God and the land around him and he notices that many families have established a homestead.

The preacher gets a happy look on his face and smiles. "You worry too much." He pats Bill on the back. "Now let's help this family find a place for tonight." Bill looks at the preacher with frustration and throws his hands up. He tosses the pick fork into the hay. Preacher Brent starts walking a little and looks back at Bill and waved him on. "Come on, you know I need you to help me with building some shelter for the Gomez family."

Mike hears Bill and Preacher Brent talk in the distance. Bill continues walking and talking as he realizes that Preacher Brent never mentioned his proposal to Sister Elizabeth. "It seems you keep taking care of everybody else's lives.

So what happened to you asking Elizabeth for her hand? Then you two could be able to begin a new life together." Preacher Brent rubs his chin with a curious look and says, "You know I'm glad you brought that up. I mean. I was asking her. Then all of a sudden, there they were." Amused Bill laughs. "There they were, huh. You keep waiting and somebody else is going steal her away from you. Ms. Elizabeth is a fine woman. She really cares about you."

The troubled preacher starts pacing back and forth. "I know. Am I doing the right thing asking her to live a life with a man who has given his heart to the Lord's service?" Bill looks him up and down. "The Good Book says it's good for a man and a woman to marry. So, I think the good Lord wants you to have somebody to take care of you too." The sound of rustling grass beats the air as Elizabeth walks up on Bill and the preacher.

Elizabeth calls out, to the preacher. "The Gomez family want you to say a prayer of blessing for their new home." With an inquisitive look she says, "What were you two talking about? Did I interrupt something?" Bill appears to be embarrassed and his face shows it. "No, No. I need to get on with my work."

Bill looks at the preacher as he tries to hurry off. "Preacher, I can talk to you more later. I don't want to stop you from your work." The preacher changes his tone and begins to stutter a little as Elizabeth looks at them both with suspicion. "Ah yes, I'm sorry, I guess we did get carried away. I was just telling Bill how we need to think about getting some of the men to help us with building the Gomez family a home."

Elizabeth looks at Preacher Brent with disbelief. "Ok, I don't know what is going on here, but I'm going to get to the bottom of it soon." She puts her hands on her hips and pats a foot. Bill appears uncomfortable and the sound shows in his voice as he speaks in an unconvincing tone. He declares, "I don't know what you are talking about Ms. Elizabeth. "Alright Bill, you're hiding something but that's fine. Truth has a way of coming out sooner or later."

She motions to the preacher with her hand. "Come on preacher, the Gomez children will be sleeping soon." Preacher Brent has a funny look on his face. "Honestly, I don't know what you are talking about." Elizabeth looks at him sternly and asserts, "You're a preacher, remember? I can't believe how you act when you get around Bill sometimes."

He proclaims in a slightly high-pitch voice, "How am I acting? Bill is my very good friend, that is all," Elizabeth smirks at him as she looks up at him. "I know, but when you get together, you are like two young boys kidding around." Preacher Brent uncomfortably continues to deny everything. "I must say I don't know what you mean Sister Elizabeth." Elizabeth touches his hand assuring him it's okay. "Brent, it doesn't matter. I'm glad you have him. You need someone you can get comfortable with from time to time. He's a good man.

The Gomez family are waiting though." Preacher Brent and Elizabeth walk up on the Gomez family as they get ready for the night. The moonlight is shining down on their tent pitched near a serene grassy area with towering green trees. In the distance, Rosita and Inez are settled down inside their tent. A campfire is burning bright with orange and yellow colors showing in the light of the fire.

The sound of the embers burning, and the pops and snaps of logs are heard through the air as an owl is hooting in the distance. Francisco proclaims, "We ain't never had a proper church to go to let alone a preacher. So, my Misses asked if you would just say a few words of blessing to celebrate our new homestead?"

The preacher pats him on the back. "Brother Francisco, I would be honored. Let's bow our heads and pray." All of them bow their heads and hold hands in a circle around the fire. The preacher begins to pray as the crackling fire burns; a reflection of flames show on their clothes.

He begins to pray. "God above, bless the Gomez family. They are good folks Lord, and they want to thank you for giving them a home. Let them receive much fruit and fertile soil to grow all your bounty. In Jesus precious name Amen."

THE SERVICE, THE SHOWDOWN, AND THE LETDOWN

It is Sunday morning, and the church is full to the brim. This is a beautiful white church with a wood cross painted on the roof of the building. The interior is charming with wood floors, and there is a stunning oak podium in front of a gold cross that is hung on the wall. The podium is surrounded by a table covered by an elegant white lace table cloth adorned with gold candle holders. The church is packed with women and men dressed in their Sunday best.

Elizabeth and Preacher Brent are teaching Sunday School to church members. "Who remember the story of the prodigal son?" Bellows Elizabeth to the congregation. Preacher Brent stands to answer the question. "I know!" Exclaims Preacher Brent. Elizabeth walks over and puts her hand on him motioning for him to be seated. "Well, wouldn't it be cheating if our very own preacher answered the question?"

The Church members in unison all exclaim, "Indeed!" Sister Francis raises her hand and answers. "I know. The story is about a young man who was bored with the life he was living with his father and wanted to go out on his own. Have fun and make his own way in the world."

The Barnabys sit in a pew a few rows back. Bill Barnaby stands and replies. "Yeah, and the father gave his son a share of the inheritance and he took it and went on his way." Matt sits between his mother and father. Alice takes Bills hat off as he stands. Bill looks over at Alice and continues speaking. "Yes, and he spent all his money on riotous living and found himself eating with pigs."

Elizabeth walks up in front of the church looking out at everyone. "Wow, you all have been listening! I am so impressed. I guess you had a good teacher." Everyone laughs. "Okay, so why don't we ask our preacher what the outcome of the story was?" The preacher responds jokily. "Oh, I can speak now." I thought I was being replaced. Everyone laughs. He walks in front of the church and stands next to Sister Elizabeth. "

Well, the prodigal son came to his senses and realized that he could be eating better at his father's table, and he decided to go home to his family." Sister Francis raises her hand. The preacher motions to her to speak. " Wasn't there a problem? I mean didn't his brother get upset about him returning."

Angelica Gomez stands and speaks. "Yeah, he couldn't believe that after all his brother had done wrong that his father would just take him back like that. He felt like he should receive some punishment or something." Elizabeth nods her head in agreement as she looks up the scripture in her Bible. "Yes, he said his son was with him and had a chance to experience the life of the Lord. He told him that they should rejoice because the brother who had gone away and done wrong, was lost and he was found.

So, they should rejoice because God had saved his brother who was lost in sin." Preacher Brent finishes telling the Bible story to the congregation with a look of gratification of his congregation learning God's word. "Well, Sister Elizabeth is right. And they had a tremendous feast to celebrate the return of the lost son and put the ring on his finger.

There is a message in this story, and it is that of forgiveness. Well let's end our service here today," entreats Preacher Brent. It is Monday afternoon, and the saloon girls are standing in front of the saloon, welcoming the cowboys. The sound of the piano wafts out into the street.

Mike McCray walks up to look over the door to see the townspeople moving about. Alice Barnaby and Francis Barnes walk past the saloon talking. As they talk, Mike is looking on and listening to their conversation. Sister Francis carries a carpet bag with some items to dress up the church. "You know the preacher and Sister Elizabeth have been spending a lot of time together.

Don't you think it's about time for him to ask for her hand? I don't rightly know." Alice has a handful of Bibles she is carrying to place in the church. "I mean, I think when the preacher is ready, he will ask her. Bill revealed to me that the preacher plans to ask Elizabeth for her hand so they can begin a life together." Sister Francis replies, "He best do something soon. All that time they are spending together, folks are bound to start talking."

Mike McCray overhears what they are discussing and is not happy with it. McCray angrily storms out of the saloon doors and walks right between Alice and Sister Francis. He is headed toward the church. Sister Francis asks in a frightful voice. "Oh, my what have we done?" Alice replies, "I didn't know he was interested in Elizabeth! I mean she can't stand McCray.

Well, he has been after her since before she went back east to teacher's college." They quicken their pace down the street. The hurried sound of their shoes hitting the ground echoes in the air. Alice replies, "what do you think he's going to do?" Sister Francis states, "I think we should warn the preacher." They cross over to the church where the preacher and some of the members are still congregating but they are too late.

Mike has gotten to the church and pounds on the door. Preacher Brent comes out to see what is going on. Sister Francis and Alice look shocked as Mike McCray approaches Preacher Brent. Mike McCray walks up to Preacher Brent and starts yelling. "Preacher, we need to talk now!" The church members hear him and start coming out to see what the commotion is.

Preacher Brent opens the door and walks out to speak to Mike. "I tried talking to you, Mr. McCray, and we could not come to an agreement about how this territory should be." Mike responds, "I don't want to talk about those outlanders! I want to know what your intentions are for Ms. Elizabeth!" Preacher Brent replies, "I don't think that is any business of yours, Mike.

" An agitated look comes over Mike's face as if he is about to explode. "You don't think it's any business of mine? I have known her since grade school. You come into town and turn her head away from me." Preacher Brent responds, "Mike, I didn't know you ever courted her at all." Mike looks around at the church members. "Everyone here knows how I feel about her." Sarcastically, the preacher looks around at the members and smiles. "Well, how come everyone knows you want to marry her except Elizabeth?"

Mike appears disturbed and a little embarrassed. "She knows, I mean she will know. I will ask her." A stern look comes over the preacher's face. "Mike, If you are sincere about your feelings for her, I will step aside. I love Elizabeth and if you don't make your feeling known to her, I am going to ask her for her hand. You have until sundown tomorrow to ask her".

A look of frustration comes over Mike's face. Mike beats his hand against his gun as he thinks. "I'll ask her, you just keep your place." Mike McCray walks off quickly toward the saloon and gets on his horse and rides through the town. Townspeople are walking about the town going into stores, the diner, and the hotel.

Sounds of children are heard playing near the school. Elizabeth is walking up the street with books heading to the schoolhouse. Mike McCray rides toward the schoolhouse to meet Elizabeth; all of a sudden, he turns around and goes to the saloons. Later that same day, Elizabeth is reading a book standing on the outside of the general store. After leaving the saloon, Mike starts rehearsing what he wants to say to Elizabeth.

Mike shouts out to himself. "Okay, what am I going to say to her." As Mike walks back and forth, practicing aloud what he will say to Elizabeth, he sees her in the distance standing near the general store reading. People walking by find him strange as he speaks to himself aloud. As he practices his dialog, he feels more confident. "Elizabeth, I know you might think this is crazy, but let's get hitched. No! He hits himself in the head and stomps his foot. That sounds stupid. I got to remember I am talking to a learned woman here". He continues talking to himself in an excited tone.

"Elizabeth, I love you, will you marry me!" As Mike stands practicing his speech, townspeople walk down the street, stopping to talk to him. One townsperson waves his hand eagerly to get his attention. "Hi, Mr. McCray!" Mighty fine weather we are having.

Mike appears bothered by them, but he speaks as he brushes them away with his hand. "Yeah, Yeah, Mighty fine." McCray is preoccupied with walking across the street to get to Elizabeth. Another townsperson comes up to him and pats him on the back and speaks. "Morning." McCray is hoping the street will clear so that he can be alone with Elizabeth. He replies to the townsperson. "Morning!" with frustration.

The town's person looks at him strangely not knowing why he was so abrupt. Mike comes close to Elizabeth, and she seems to be intently reading her book. Mike waves his hand in front of her face to get her attention. "Morning Ms. Elizabeth." Mike seems to stumble with his words. She looks up from her book casually and speaks in a disinterested tone. "Good morning to you sir."

She looks back down at her book. He stands there, almost frozen with fear. "I, I was wondering if." — He hesitates. He takes his hat off. He continues to speak in a humble voice. "Well, I was wondering if you might have…" He swallows nervously. "Have a moment or two to speak with me." Elizabeth looks at him inquisitively and replies. "I don't know, I am just about to head to the schoolhouse."

She turns to walk away. He rushes after her and touches her coat. Mike says, "Please I just want to tell you I am so sorry. I mean. About your pa and all, I mean, how hard I worked him. You know, my head is hard as iron. I mean I can be bout stubborn as a mule." With a surprised look on her face, Elizabeth replies, "I don't know what to say. I never thought the day would come when you would apologize for anything."

Her voice shows compassion as her eyes well up with forgiveness; she pulls her book close to her chest. "Mr. McCray, I forgive you. I should not have held such a grudge anyway. That's not the Christian way. I am sorry. You did my heart well telling me that." She grabs his hands cupping them in hers. "Thank you. Thank you so much."

Mike is fumbling nervously with his belt. Mike kicks at the dirt trying to get the words he wants to say fastened in his mind. "Well, I was hoping…" She cuts him off as she is getting her books together. "I am so sorry; I have to hurry now and get to the schoolhouse, the children are waiting. Thank you so much. I realize now that maybe we can be civil and maybe even friends after all."

He gets a sober look on his face as if he realizes he should not ask her to marry him. In a solemn voice, he replies, "Well, thank you for your time, ma'am." He puts his hat back on." She puts her hand out to shake his hand again. "God bless you." He shakes her hand, and he turns and walks toward the saloon.

WEDDING, BIRTH, TRUTH, AND
FRIENDSHIP

On this sunny day, the church is full of flowers, indicating a wedding is taking place. Church members are seated as Elizabeth and Preacher Brent are exchanging their vows. Elizabeth and Preacher Brent had a beautiful wedding service with rose pedals thrown in the air as they leave the church. Sister Francis is misty as she speaks to Elizabeth. "This is such a wonderful day! I am so excited for you both. To think I was the one who introduced you. It seems like yesterday when Preacher Brent came to Red Springs."

Church members are exiting the sanctuary to see Sister Elizabeth and Preacher Brent leave for their honeymoon. Matt Barnaby nudges his Dad and starts whispering. "If they don't stop her from talking, they will never get to their honeymoon." He laughs. Bill replies, "Yeah, she can go on a bit." Alice admonishes them as she hears what Matt is saying to Bill; she tells them to show some consideration.

"What are you two talking about? Be nice, Sister Francis is just happy for the newlyweds." Brent looks around at everyone, with Elizabeth on his arm, with a joyful expression on his face. "This town has been good to me. You all welcomed me and believed in me.

Now I have married one of the most beautiful charming, educated women in Red Springs! " Elizabeth looks at him with admiration and waves her handkerchief as she speaks. "Do go on preacher." Everyone laughs. Preacher Brent rears back and continues talking as he grabs her arm. "Well, it may have taken me a while to ask this lady for her hand, but you best be sure, I will never let her leave my side from this day forward."

There is a resounding sound of oohs and ah's coming from the crowd. Some of the women are touched by what he says and take out a handkerchief to wipe their eyes. Then Bill begins to clap and everyone joins in. Matt pulls at the preacher's coat to get his attention. "Preacher, I have a question for you, when are you two going to get on down the road? I'm sure you and Sister Elizabeth would like to spend some time alone now that you done said your wedding vows and all."

The Preacher and Elizabeth approach their green wagon drawn by two beautiful Clydesdale horses. The wagon is decorated with fresh-cut yellow and white daisies and pink lilies with bright white ribbons to symbolize the purity of this union. Elizabeth wears a charming off-white lace gown.

Preacher Brent pats Matt on the head and replies. "Matt, you are right. I tell you, Bill, that boy of yours, he is a smart one. Let's get on down the road Mrs. Carson." As he spins her around, her lovely white laced gown waves in the wind as he lifts her onto the wagon. She is overcome by his exuberant and gentle affection. Elizabeth looks him in the eye with affection. "I do declare, Mr. Carson, I never knew you were so strong.

The preacher then gets onto the wagon sitting up with great pride and love. Well, Ma'am, I never had such a delicate package to load on this here wagon before." He kisses her. Bill is smiling from ear-to-ear bursting with happiness for them both. "Congratulations you two. It's been a long time coming!" Alice is overcome with emotion and turns and looks at her husband and replies. "Oh, Bill, at least he finally asked her. You settle down and remember how long it took you to ask me."

The Preacher looks surprised as he wonders how Bill may have proposed to Alice. "I don't think I ever heard that story about how Bill proposed." He smiles. In a sarcastic tone, Bill responds." And you never will. Gone get on up the road with your new bride." An emotional but happy Elizabeth looks at them and smiles.

" You two always playing around. Bill and Alice, we thank you both so much." Sister Francis walks over and touches her friend's hand joyfully to show her approval. "Oh, Elizabeth, you just look so beautiful." Tears of joy stream down Elizabeth's face as she reaches out to touch her friend, Sister Francis' hand while she is saying goodbye. The preacher looks at them both. He says, "My Lord, we better go before all the ladies start to be whaling." Elizabeth hits him on the arm with fondness.

"Oh, you. I'm just so happy." He kisses her. Preacher Brent squeezes her hand. "Me too." They ride off down the road which is lined with enchanting trees curved inward making a beautiful tunnel of leaves as they ride off. All the church members are waving goodbye as the wagon goes up the road with ribbons and flowers dragging on the ground as they ride away.

Years later, a beautiful farmhouse sits surrounded by green grass and beautiful fruit trees gleaming with ripe fruit. Chickens are running around in the distance on the farm and a few pigs are making noise in a nearby pen. The green wagon that the Preacher and Elizabeth drove off in sits in the barn.

Three horses are lined up in the barn stalls. Bill and Alice drive up quickly. "Whoa, Whoa" Bill calls out to the horses. He and Alice get off their wagon quickly. They rush up to the farmhouse and start knocking on the door. Preacher Brent opens the door. I am so glad you are here. She has been aching for a while. Alice says, "I will go right in and tend to her." She carries in some blankets and a wash basin.

Preacher Brent and Bill remain on the porch. The preacher is nervously pacing back and forth in a distressful manner. Bill looks surprised that the preacher is so nervous. "I never thought I would see our preacher unravel before my eyes. You're about to fall apart Brent. Come on, she is going to be alright. The birthing of a baby is an exciting time."

A voice of worry and concern come from Preacher Brent as he speaks. "I'm excited Bill, but this is the first time in my life I have felt so helpless. She's aching so much." "Brent, I have birthed just about all the babies in this here settlement and they are all doing just fine. Now you trust me. Elizabeth will be just fine." Preacher Brent takes a deep breath and blows it out.

"I know what you say is true. Lord help me to get myself together. I just love that woman so much. I can't stand to see her in any pain." Elizabeth suffers as the labor pains are coming faster and faster. Alice puts a cloth in the bowl and wrings it out and then Alice wipes Elizabeth's face. Elizabeth starts breathing harder and harder.

She begins screaming out. Alice runs down the steps and rushes out to the door and finds Bill and Preacher Brent still talking. Alice walks out on the porch and stomps her foot to get their attention. "You fellows going to talk all day or are we going to birth this baby! She is ready now, come on Bill." Bill turns to the preacher and says, "I got to go now, you settle down preacher. God won't let no harm come to Elizabeth."

Bill goes into the room and closes the door. Alice goes in and the preacher goes out on the porch and gets on his knees and prays. Preacher Brent looks to heaven and starts to pray. "Dear Lord, I know you are a merciful God. I know that women have pain when they are having babies. But if you can see fit that my Elizabeth doesn't have such a hard time, I will be forever grateful."

The sound of a smack fills the room as the cry of the baby pierces through as the sound travels outside. Bill and Alice run out to get the preacher in from the porch to see the baby. The Preacher has a concerned look as Bill gives him the news. The preacher looks at them both and waves his arms in the air as he speaks. "Well, is she alright?" Bill replies. "It's a boy! A healthy baby boy." A delightful look appears on Alice's face as she gazes at the preacher. "Oh, he is such a beautiful little thing."

Preacher Brent claps his hands together with glee. "A boy! Oh my, how is Elizabeth?" Bill replies. "You can see her, and the baby now, come on." They all run into the house and the door slams behind them. Bill puts his hand on Preacher Brent's chest as he walks in to calm him a little. "Now take it easy, she is still very tired." Preacher Brent walks into the bedroom and looks elated.

Brent looks over toward the bed and Elizabeth is lying there with the baby next to her. Preacher Brent slowly walks toward them. Preacher Brent touches the baby's finger gently. "Are you alright?" Elizabeth's brow is filled with perspiration, and her face is somewhat red as she speaks. "I am fine Brent. Don't you worry. I'm just a bit worn out."

The baby is a beautiful pink hue. It is a baby boy with just a hint of red hair. She has him wrapped in a white and blue blanket with a lace trim she made from her wedding gown. She holds him close to her bosom rubbing her cheek on his soft head. Preacher Brent begins to stroke her head. She speaks in a soft voice to the preacher. He rubs on the blanket as he looks at his son. "He's so little and so attractive. He almost looks like a girl. He looks like you Elizabeth."

She smiles at her son as she looks over at him. "He is beautiful for a boy, isn't he? But I think he looks just like his Daddy." Preacher Brent touches his son's little arm as he speaks. "You do?" He smiles. "Well, I guess he does that indeed." Alice and Bill stand in the doorway of the bedroom looking on, beaming with happiness for the Preacher and Elizabeth. Alice replies, "What are you going to name him?"

Preacher and Elizabeth look at each other and then look at the baby. Elizabeth touches the baby's face once again as she speaks. "I think I would like to call him Joshua." Elizabeth looks over at the preacher for his approval. Bill stands proud and happy. "Joshua, I think that's a fine name. Like Joshua in the Bible."

Alice nudges Bill as she squints at him with a funny look on her face. She replies, "You hush up and let the preacher decide on the name for his baby." Preacher Brent walks to the other side of the bed and holds Elizabeth's hand as he looks over at Bill. "Joshua is a fine name. A good strong name for a boy. Joshua is the one that helped Moses leading the children of Israel through the wilderness. That's a fine name for my son."

Elizabeth replies. "I am glad you like it. I know now since you are commencing to quoting scripture and all that, you really feel good about his name." Bill looks around the room and hurriedly starts collecting his things and putting them into his bag. "Come on woman, let's get home and let them enjoy their little one. Joshua, yeah, I like that name very well."

Alice throws her hands up and responds in a sarcastic tone, "I know you just want to get home and eat." Bill looks at her. "After all this work, shouldn't I be hungry?" Alice replies, "What work? Elizabeth did all the work. You just caught the baby!" She laughs as they walk out. Preacher Brent is holding the baby as Elizabeth is sleeping.

THE PAIN OF PREJUDICE AND IGNORANCE

While riding into Red Springs, Mike McCray surveys the town as he passes by the saloon, hotel, diner, and the church in the distance. Mike comes up on the schoolhouse and sees Elizabeth teaching the class. He stops, gets off his horse, and looks through the window for a moment. Mike's eyes fill with admiration as he looks at Elizabeth.

Suddenly, he gets a sad expression over his face; he turns away, climbs on his horse and rides off toward the saloon. The white schoolhouse sits in a very pleasant location with a pond and trees and flowers in front that Elizabeth planted with the children. The schoolhouse has a sawdust floor and rows of wooden desks attached to chairs, as well as a blackboard at the front of the room. Elizabeth's desk is adorned with flowers, a bright red apple, and schoolbooks.

The children are attentive as Elizabeth is teaching and she is beginning her lesson in spelling with Mary, a cute little girl with blonde pigtails sitting in front with a lovely pink dress. Jimmy, an older farm boy, has on his overalls and brown boots and his clothes are worn and tattered. Ann, who is a skinny girl with fiery red hair, has on a bright yellow dress which is as bright as her personality.

Ann is a very smart girl but sometimes she gets a little too sassy. The town store is owned by Ann's parents, and she loves to read books from around the world. As Elizabeth is writing on the board, she turns to begin asking the children to spell the words. "Today, I am going to have you spell some words from our list that we did the other day. Okay, let's start with Mary. Please, spell Cat and use it in a sentence." Mary stands and looks at the class and speaks. "Cat. C-A-T. The cat went up the road."

Elizabeth replies. "Very good Mary! Mary smiles and sits back down. Let's have Jimmy do the next one. Horse." Jimmy stands with his head down. Jimmy pauses and then replies. "H-O-R-S-E. H-A-R-S-E. I ride the harse on my land." The children all laugh. Ann stands and replies. "It's H-O-R- S-E, you so stupid!"

Elizabeth taps her ruler on her desk. "Now, that wasn't nice Ann. You apologize to Jimmy." Ann turns and licks her tongue at Jimmy. "But he never can spell anything right. He doesn't belong here. He doesn't know nothing." The children laugh again. Elizabeth taps her ruler firmer on her desk to settle the class. "Now Jimmy came from another town where they didn't have schooling like you do.

So, you should say you are sorry, or you will have to stand in the corner." Ann eyes roll to the back of her head as she speaks through clenched teeth. "I'm sorry, Ms. Elizabeth. I didn't mean to say that." Elizabeth sits down as she speaks. "I know you didn't. Let's take a break and go outside and play for a little bit." The noise of the children moving their desk and running out to play fills the room. The children are outside playing and talking.

Jimmy stays behind at his desk writing on his chalkboard. Elizabeth is in the front of the class cleaning the blackboard and putting books back on the shelves. Elizabeth turns and sees that Jimmy is still sitting with his head down writing on his chalkboard. She walks over to him and taps him on the shoulder. "Don't you want to go out and play with the other children?"

Jimmy looks up at Elizabeth as he speaks. "No Ma'am. I just need to work on my words." She sits down in a chair beside Jimmy. "Ok. Well, I will stay here and help you." Jimmy smiles as he speaks. "Mrs. Elizabeth, you are one of the nicest people in town." She hugs him for a moment. "Thank you, Jimmy. I like you too."

The town is busy with townspeople moving around getting food and going into the town stores and working. Mike McCray rides up and sees some of the men from town standing by the McCray mining office while a storekeeper is putting things out on display. The bank office is just opening and some townspeople are heading into the bank to do business.

Mike rides over to the men who are milling about and speaks to them. "Hey, fellows, how are you doing?" Benny replies. "Just getting ready to head over to the saloon and see some of the girls," Mike replies. "A little early for that isn't it?" Benny responds. "No. I just been having a hard day. Thought I would have a few." Mike looks over toward the saloon and sees the doors are open. "You know, maybe you're right. I got a few things on my mind too."

Mike rides over to the saloon and ties up his horse. The men walk over and enter the saloon together. Although it is early, the saloon girls are busy preparing the saloon for customers while some men are starting a card game. A Saloon girl sees Mike McCray and his men coming in, she calls out. "Hey, what you fellows doing in here this early?" Another Saloon girl replies. "You fellows looking for trouble this early."

Mike laughs as he speaks. "Just thought I would get in a game with the fellows." A card player looks as he hears Mike talking. "We just playing a few hands, nothing serious." Mike walks over and sits down. "Doesn't have to be serious. We can play a few hands for fun fellows." Another card player is shuffling the deck. "Whatever you say, Mike." May sees them gathering and shouts out. "You fellows need something to drink over there?"

Another Saloon girl walks over to the bar when May is standing as she speaks. "May, I'm tired; I think I'm going to head up." May replies." Okay. We will be fine." Mike taps the table to signal he needs more cards. "Give me two cards." Another card player motions to the dealer. "I need one." The other card player replies. "I'll take one." Mike looks over at the piano. "Hey, let's get some music playing over here." May taps the piano player on the shoulder.

"Okay Mike, it's a little early though." The piano player starts playing; the sound of music covers the room. As Mike smokes a cigar, the room is filled with the smell of cigar smoke. The card player looks puzzled when Mike puts his hand on the table and throws the cards down. "Deal me out, fellows."

Mike gets up and walks over to the window. The card player replies. "Okay Mike, no problem." They watch Mike as he seems to be preoccupied with what he is looking at through the saloon window. Mike sees Preacher Brent go into the land office. A while later, the preacher comes out with some papers in his hand and tuck them into his vest pocket. Mike's face fills with anger as he continues to look out as the Preacher walks away.

Michael observes townspeople walking around and cowboys riding through town. Looking through the window, he sees people walking over to the diner, and he notices people eating from the diner window. May and the saloon girls sit around watching the card game. It's still a little early and they are just talking with a couple of card players. The game has gotten quite interesting when Mike returns to the table later in the day.

The men are laughing and enjoying the game as the piano music wafts into the street. During the last few minutes of the school day, the children pack up as Elizabeth stands at the door. She says goodbye to the children as they leave with their books and belongings in their hands.

In the schoolhouse, Jimmy sits at his desk while Elizabeth walks outside and watches the other children leave. "Goodbye. See you tomorrow!" All the children wave as they go down the road toward home. "Goodbye Mrs. Carson." Elizabeth walks back inside and sees Jimmy still at his desk. "Jimmy, why are you still here?"

Jimmy replies, "Ms. Elizabeth, if I tell you something, will you keep it a secret?" "Yes. But why do I have to keep it a secret?" He puts his head down as if he is ashamed and then looks up at her. "Cause my Maw doesn't want us to bother anybody with our problems. But she is sick." Elizabeth rubs his hand to comfort him. "Well, how about I take you home after I clean up some things and check on your Ma?" Jimmy looks up at her with a brightness in his eyes. "Yes, Ma'am. I think that would be fine."

Preacher Brent and Bill are picking up supplies at the local store in Red Springs. Bill loads the wagon when Preacher Brent notices Elizabeth and Jimmy walking across the street. Elizabeth and Jimmy appear to be in a hurry when Bill looks over and notices them as well.

"I wonder where Ms. Elizabeth is going with the Mitchell boy." A concerned look comes over Preacher Brent's face. "I don't know. It's supper time; she should be heading home to the boys." "Can you hold up a minute?" Bill keeps loading the wagon. "I'll just finish loading." The preacher walks over toward Elizabeth and Jimmy. "Elizabeth where are you going this time of day?"

In a determined voice, Elizabeth speaks to the preacher. "Oh, I was just helping Jimmy. His Ma is a little under the weather and I was just going to see what I could do to help." Bill comes over with the wagon and overhears them talking. The preacher hears distress in Elizabeth's voice. "Well, why don't let me and Bill drive you over to the Mitchell's home and maybe Bill can tend to her."

Bill stares at the preacher puzzled because everyone knows about the Mitchells and that Mr. Mitchell works for Mike McCray. Also that Mr. Mitchell would not accept help from Bill. A scared look comes over Jimmy's face as he shouts. "No! I mean my Pa ain't going to let no Negro look at my Maw." Bill and Elizabeth look at each other as Bill climbs down from the wagon.

Preacher Brent is startled by Jimmy's response. "I see. Well, why don't you get Doc Madison to look at your Ma?" Jimmy takes off his hat and lowers his head. He says, "We don't have money for the doctor. " Elizabeth puts her arm around Jimmy. "Well, Jimmy, I let Bill Barnaby birth both my boys and treat me and Preacher Brent all the time."

Bill looks at Jimmy as he moves some of the supplies around to accommodate Jimmy getting on the wagon. Jimmy replies, "I know Ma'am. I heard about that. But my Pa would skin me alive if I brought him to our home to treat my Ma. He works for Mr. McCray and can't be seen with the likes of him." Jimmy points at Bill with a finger of disdain. A look of anger is visible on Bill's face when he piers at Jimmy.

Preacher Brent replies. "Well, Jimmy, Mrs. Carson can go inside and try and tend to your mother but, I and Mr. Bill are going to drive you over." Jimmy calms as he hears the preacher's calm voice. "Oh, ok. I guess that will be okay." The preacher helps Elizabeth onto the wagon. Bill and the preacher get onboard and Jimmy hops on the back.

Bill, Elizabeth, and Preacher look at each other. Bill pulls back on the reigns to start the horses moving. He shouts, "Ya, Ya." The horses start moving down the road. It is night now and the Preacher, Elizabeth, Jim, and Bill are heading to the Mitchell place on the prairie. They finally arrive at the Mitchell home and it is a worn-down shack of a house. The preacher helps Elizabeth down as Jimmy waits by the wagon.

Jimmy and Elizabeth go inside the house for Elizabeth to start tending to Jimmy's mother, Susan. Jimmy's mother looks gravely ill and her head is hot as fire. Elizabeth sends Jimmy to get a pan of cold water as she grabs some clothes from a nearby table and begins taring them apart. Jimmy comes back with the water as Susan Mitchell, Jimmy's mother moans in pain. Elizabeth puts the clothes in the cold water and puts them on Susan's head to cool her temperature.

Mrs. Mitchell is red with fever and appears to be in a lot of pain. Time is passing and the Preacher and Bill begin to get concerned about Elizabeth. The preacher goes to knock on the door to check to see if everything is alright. Jimmy's father, Joe Mitchell comes to the door and sees the preacher outside with Bill.

"You are that preacher that I heard about with that "darkee" as a friend." An expression of uneasiness appears on the preacher's face as he speaks. "Mr. Mitchell. I don't know what kind of man you are, but I let my wife come and help your wife cause I'm a Godly man. But I'm not going to stand here and let you insult Bill Barnaby, he's a good man." Bill has a shocked look on his face, and he turns and gets back on the wagon which is right near the front door as the preacher keeps talking to Joe Mitchell.

Joe replies. "No disrespect to you. I know what you and your wife have done for folks around here. I know about him too. But I don't cotton to a Negro looking after a white woman as her doctor." Preacher Brent moves back and speaks in a strong firm tone. "Mr. Mitchell, I think we best be going. Can you call my wife?"

Joe looks back and, in the distance, a dim light shows Elizabeth by the beside of Mrs. Mitchell trying to tend to her. Joe opens the door and calls out to Elizabeth. "I will. Thank you kindly for your help. Ma'am, you best be going." Elizabeth walks up to Joe and speaks to him in a worried tone. "Your wife is very sick. You really need to get her to a doctor." He says, "I'm sure you did all you could Ma'am."

Elizabeth replies. "More can be done." Joe says, "If you mean by him…" as he points abruptly to Bill on the wagon. "… no Ma'am. She will be fine." Later Preacher, Elizabeth, and Bill take the ride back to the Carson farm. It is so silent; all that can be heard is the sound of the wagon wheel and the horse's hooves on the ground. The road is dark and only the moonlight is shining to guide them as the sound of the night surrounds them.

All of them are struck with an unbearable silence as they ride toward the preacher's home. Preacher Brent turns and looks at Bill and Elizabeth as he speaks. "This silence is killing me!" Somebody please says something. Bill looks frustrated and almost explodes as he answers. "I'll say it! Ain't nothing changed around here in all this time. I've done birthed babies, mended folks and everything and there is still folk that feel like Joe Mitchell."

Elizabeth throws up her hands and shakes her head in irritation. "He's right. I mean. I couldn't believe that man would sure as let his wife die than have Bill give her something to cure her." As the preacher listens to the horrifying story of another man's views harming his family's health, a look of despair appears on his face.

"I don't know what to say. I just thought that if they saw you could do these things, folks would change." Bill puts his hand on the preacher's shoulder to show he supports him. "Some folks have, at least the ones who are in our community. But those folks in town, they all have the same mindset as McCray." Elizabeth sighs with despair. "All the prayers in the world haven't changed that man in all this time."

Bill jerks the reigns to stop the wagon. "I'm not saying what you are doing isn't a good thing preacher. But you got to accept everybody doesn't think like you." Preacher Brent starts to climb down from the wagon and his statue looks as if he is beaten down from disappointment. "I guess that's a lesson the good Lord wants to teach me." Preacher Brent looks defeated as he walks off on the road, away from his house.

Elizabeth stays on the wagon and talks to Bill for a moment. Bill whispers to her to ensure the preacher doesn't hear him. "The preacher looks disappointed about what happened tonight. But that's how the world is for people like me." Elizabeth touches his hand to show she sympathizes with him.

"Bill, you must understand, he's a man that wants the world to be a better place. So, it hurts him when he sees his hands are tied." Bill replies, "Ms. Elizabeth, Preacher Brent has done my family a good service. He taught me that a white man can be different than the McCray's out here." A solemn look appears on Elizabeth's face as she speaks. "Maybe you should tell him that some time. It's hard to fight for causes that seem lost all the time without getting a little down."

Bill speaks in a joking tone with a forced smile on his face. "Well, I didn't say it was a lost cause. Maybe a little hard but I hope not lost." A feeling of warmth is heard in Elizabeth's voice as she speaks. "I see why Brent likes you so much. She smiles and touches his shoulder. You can take any situation and make him smile. I'm glad you are in our lives."

Bill pulls back on the reigns to keep the horses still. "I reckon, I'm partial to you both myself." Bill puts his hand out to help Elizabeth down from the wagon. "Good night, Bill." She walks into the house and Bill tips his hat to her as he rides off.

TWO DIFFERENT FAMILIES

Five years later, the preacher and Elizabeth are riding into town for a church fair with their sons, Joshua and Jonah. Everyone gets off at the church, where church members are already gathered. Children are running around, playing, and many families are sitting on blankets with food while some adults are playing horseshoes. Joshua and Jonah run over to play with the children and are excited as they see several cowboys doing tricks with horses.

Some other men are just talking and whittling wood figures for the children. Later that day, in the open country, Preacher Brent, Elizabeth, Joshua, and Jonah are riding home and enjoying the breeze as they pass through the beautiful green prairie. Preacher Brent turns to Elizabeth and speaks with enthusiasm. "That sure was a fine day, wasn't it? Sister Francis made a fine apple pie."

Elizabeth replies. "Yeah, I saw you made sure you ate more than your fill of it." Joshua replies. "I didn't taste any but, Sister Alice made some good biscuits and beans. I'm stuffed. Look at my stomach, it's just as big as yours, Pa." Jonah replies, "Ma, I liked all the food you made. I didn't care about any of those other ladies' food."

Elizabeth looks over at Jonah and smiles and rubs his face gently with her hand and Jonah looks at her lovingly. "Well, thank you, Jonah. I'm glad one of the Carson men enjoyed my cooking." The preacher gets a look of guilt on his face and pulls back on the reigns of the horses as they are riding on the road toward their land. " Now, I wasn't saying you don't make good food. I just never said it was one of your best talents."

Joshua touches her hand as he speaks. "I love your food, Ma. I don't know what Pa is talking about." The preacher looks at both of his sons and realizes they are soothing their mother about her food and has left him to take a tongue lashing. Elizabeth looks over at the preacher as she speaks. "It looks like you are on your own preacher. Only the good Lord can get you out of this one."

The preacher smiles and sits up on the seat. He winks his eye at his son Joshua and clears his throat. "Well, there are a lot better things in this world than being the best cook. Being the most beautiful and smartest woman in town counts for a lot more than some old pie." He looks at Joshua and Jonah and nods his head and Elizabeth smiles.

Elizabeth reaches over and holds the preacher's hand and looks at him with a kind look on her face. "I think you may have gotten yourself out of a scolding this time. But next time we have a church gathering, you better dote on my vitals like you do Sister Francis', ya hear!" She moves close to the preacher and lays her head on his shoulder. Jonah lays his head on Elizabeth's lap as she rubs his hair gently.

Preacher Brent pulls back on the reigns as he speaks. "I certainly will." The sound of the horse's feet on the road lull Jonah to sleep. The preacher pulls up to their house. Jonah is now asleep in Elizabeth's lap, curled up like a ball. Preacher Brent reaches out to Elizabeth as he speaks. "Give him to me and I will put him to bed."

Elizabeth pulls down Jonah's shirt gently as she gives him to the preacher. "No, you take him in. I'll put him to bed." Preacher Brent takes Jonah softly, trying not to wake him as he speaks to Joshua. "Joshua, unhitch the horses and put the wagon away," the preacher commanded. Joshua replies, "Yes, sir." Joshua unhitches the horses from the wagon and walks the horses away toward the barn.

Preacher and Elizabeth walk up the steps and Elizabeth starts putting Jonah to bed and lays him down and covers him up, placing a soft kiss on his forehead and tenderly wiping his hair away from his eyes. Joshua comes into the room clicking his boots together trying to get the mud off. The sound of him hitting the boots causes Elizabeth to quiet him. "Careful, you don't wake your brother. Joshua replies, "I won't Ma."

Joshua starts taking off his clothes and putting on his night shirt. Elizabeth looks over at Joshua as he is folding his clothes. "Good night son." Elizabeth closes the door as he puts the clothes on the chair next to his bed. Joshua climbs in the bed and blows out the candle beside his bed and goes to sleep. Preacher Brent is fast asleep, and light is burning on the table by the bed next to him.

Elizabeth sits back in a wooden rocking chair and grabs a cover and pulls it up over herself as she begins to read her Bible. After reading for a while, she climbs into bed next to the preacher and falls asleep rapidly as the moonlight glistens on the window. While Mike McCray is enjoying a cigar on his porch the next day, he hears homesteaders hammering boards as they build new homes.

In the kitchen, Martha McCray, his wife, is moving about cooking all kinds of food that is filling the house with a tasteful smell. Mike comes in to have breakfast with his son, Larcey, as Martha serves them their food. He pushes his plate across the table. "Why can't you make a decent plate of food?" As Mike tosses his food to the side and his son, Larcey looks on with a shameful expression on his face. A disappointed expression is seen on Martha's face. "I'm sorry. I'll fix you a fresh plate."

"Daddy, why are you so angry?" Larcey asks. Mike moves his chair back from the table. "I have put up with them, outlanders coming in and settling in this territory for too many years; it's time to do something about it." Larcey stands up and hits his hand on the table. "I'll take care of them outlanders for you Daddy!" Mike laughs and rubs Larcey's head. "You got a bit more growing to do for that son. Just a bit more."

Mike pats Larcey on the top of his head and He walks out onto the porch. Mike looks out at his land and sees across in the distance all the homesteader's cabins. He walks his land and looks out at his cattle and the ranch hands that are tending to the horses.

He gets on his horse and rides over toward the end of his land and looks out at the settlers walking around and farming and working. He is sitting on his horse and begins to speak aloud to himself. "Your time is coming. It's not going to be much longer for you outlanders." He jerks back on the reigns of his horse and rides off quickly toward the town.

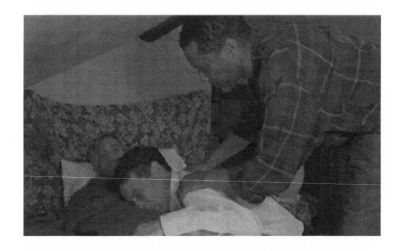

A TRAGEDY WITH CONSEQUENCES

Twelve years after growing up on the McCray ranch, Larcey stands tall with sandy brown hair and a powerful stance. Larcey looks more like his mother than his father, as he has her gentle features, but he is a handsome young man who has already learned how to run his father's ranch. Larcey runs into the house with urgency.

"Pa, one of them sheep that those outlanders had done got into our land again. And I notice that somebody been bending our fence back to be letting them out. Now they are coming on our land Pa. When are we going do something?" Mike speaks with a firm tone. "I told you boy, I would let you know." Larcey gets a look of disapproval on his face and frustration and casts his eyes to the floor in disappointment. "If you weren't so stuck on that preacher's wife then, we would have got rid of them outlanders long ago."

Mike walks up to him quickly and gets close to his son's face. Larcey's facial expression quickly changes as he sees he has angered his father. "What you say to me boy!? You better watch yourself." Mike points his finger in his face and Larcey bows his head in submission.

Larcey looks up at his father with a dissatisfied expression. "Well, I heard in town that she is sick with pneumonia, anyway bad off." Mike's gaze turns to a very concerned look as he grabs Larcey by his sleeve. "Where you hear that?" Larcey replies. "When I was at the general store, I overheard Sister Francis telling that Negro woman, Alice, that she was sick. She told her to get that healer man who is that Negro woman's husband in a hurry."

Mike starts grabbing his hat and rushes out to get the horse saddled. He hollers out to his son. "Boy, you run into town and get Doc Madison and bring em here straight away!" Larcey runs out to the porch and looks at Mike with an upset countenance on his face. "But, that ain't none of our business. Sides what would Ma think about it?" Mike keeps putting his saddle on his horse.

He comes up on the porch and opens the door and turns and looks at Larcey with a firm expression on his face. "You let me deal with your Ma. Just get and don't you come back without the Doc." Larcey gets on his horse and rides toward town and Mike walks into the house. He sees Martha standing in the parlor and she appeared displeased as she speaks.

106

"What are you doing? You know that preacher ain't going to let you near his wife. Why can't you let them be?" Mike stomps toward her and motions as if he may strike her. "Woman, you need to tend to your business. I knew that family since she was a child and her father even worked for me. I am just doing them a kindness, that's all." Martha says, "A kindness!"

He walks outside on the porch and Martha follows him. "Well, how about doing a kindness for your son. You got him so obsessed with your hate for this preacher. I'm afraid for him. All he wants to do is please you." He turns and walks up to her. "I love my son. You let me handle my son and you just tend to taking care of us."

She walks away, shaking her head as she goes into the house. It is now nighttime, and the sound of the saloon can be heard in the street. Larcey rides up to Dr. Jarvis Madison's house and starts thumping on the door as he waits for it to open; he starts knocking harder. Doctor Madison rushes to open the door grabbing his hat as he opens it. "Why you knocking so hard? Is it an emergency?"

Larcey takes his hat off to show respect. "Yes, my Pa sent me to fetch you for Sister Elizabeth, that preacher's wife." Doctor Madison gets a strange and confused look on his face. "I have never treated her before." In a hurried tone, Larcey speaks. "Doc, we don't have time to jaw. She is in a bad way with a wicked illness, her condition can worsen fast. Pa said you need to meet him at the house. It's just across from our land, just a couple of miles up."

He gets on his horse, and they ride off and end up in front of Mike's ranch in the dark of night. McCray sees them as they approach and jumps on his horse and rides off with Dr. Madison to the Carson's place. Larcey sits on his horse and watches the urgency his father shows to get to Elizabeth's bedside.

At the Carson home, Elizabeth is very ill with consumption and Alice is tending to her. She looks very weak and her skin looks gray, and Elizabeth is burning up with fever. Bill is mixing some herbs for her in a bowl and he begins to pour the mixture into a glass and tries to get Elizabeth to drink it. They raise her head to drink, and Elizabeth begins to cough and can't seem to take in the herbs.

Preacher Brent stands at the door watching as they care for her. Joshua and Jonah are not far off sitting in the outer room and they hear Elizabeth coughing. Alarmed by the sound of her coughing, they hurry to the door to see her. Jonah is pale with fear when he sees his mother. "Pa, Ma looks so weak. You think Mr. Bill can really help her?"

Jonah stares at his mother so hard his mind wanders back in a daydream thinking about Elizabeth and all the things he did with his mother. People are playing games and eating at the church outing. Elizabeth calls out to her son while he is playing. "Jonah, Jonah!" Jonah runs up to Elizabeth and she lifts him from the ground and swings him around. Jonah laughs. Jonah begins to smile for a moment and the Preacher touches Jonah's shoulder.

Suddenly, the look on Jonah's face changes and he comes out of his daydream and realizes the anguish of pain Elizabeth is feeling again. With an assuring voice, Preacher Brent speaks to Jonah. "He will do his best son. Bill is a good healer. She couldn't be in better hands. You go back to your room and say a prayer for her. Joshua, take your brother and try and get some sleep."

It is night and McCray and Dr. Madison are riding hard toward the Carson place." Preacher, Alice and Bill are all in the bedroom and Elizabeth cannot stop coughing. Alice is going back and forth to the water basin and putting clothes on Elizabeth's head while Bill, is covering Elizabeth with blankets. Elizabeth continues to look worse. Bill goes out to talk to Preacher Brent as Alice continues to take care of Elizabeth.

Preacher Brent is in the parlor pacing back and forth with a worried look on his face as Bill approaches him and touches him on his back. The preacher looks at Bill with a look of despair. "Yes." In a painful voice Bill speaks. "I have done all I can. She is so weak." Elizabeth seems to be slipping away. McCray and Doctor Madison are riding swiftly on horseback passing the homesteaders homes in the distance. The sound of the horse's hooves hitting the ground is hard and fast.

On the porch of the Carson house, Alice and Bill are talking when McCray rides up fast in the distance. Alice hurries into the house pushing Bill inside the doorway as she closes the door. Preacher Brent is inside the bedroom with Elizabeth as she is fading fast, and her face looks gray and pale.

She begins to decline, and Preacher Brent kneels beside her and lays his head on Elizabeth's chest. He stays there as the life releases from her body and Bill walks up and touches him on his back. "She is gone." Preacher Brent is overcome with grief and cries out with a hollowed sound of pain. The preacher can't speak as tears come down his eyes and he rubs Elizabeth's hair and touches her hand. Bill stands and looks at her as a tear falls from his eye while he covers Elizabeth's face.

As he watches from afar, Jonah is still frozen in place with disbelief as tears run down his face. There is a hard knocking at the door and Preacher Brent comes out of the room and Bill and Alice follow. He opens the door, and Mike pushes by the Preacher. "Hurry man, I have Doc Madison here for your wife!" Preacher Brent is wiping tears from his face that Mike did not even notice.

Preacher Brent sighs with a deep long breath of defeat. "You're too late. She is gone." He puts his head down as life has given him a hard punch in the stomach. Mike sits down on the porch almost paralyzed with astonishment. In a soft hurt voice and with a look of shock on his face, he speaks, "Gone? She can't be gone. An enchanting creature like that."

Preacher Brent touches Mike McCray on the shoulder and Mike pulls away abruptly. "We will all miss her. She is with the Almighty now." Mike jerks his body up from the porch and stares at the preacher. He yells out at him. "This is all your fault! You and your Negro healing man. What were you thinking? She needed a real doctor. Why didn't you get Doc Madison from town?"

Preacher Brent replies, "Bill did his best. He did all that could be done for her. Doc Madison could not have done any better." In a sad troubled voice, Doctor Madison speaks, "I'm sure I could have done something more. But it is a shame for sure. She was a lovely woman with a beautiful spirit; she will be missed." Preacher Brent replies. "I know you believe you could have done better. But I trust that…"

Mike cuts him off in an angry frustrated voice. "Hush up! The woman is dead, what does it matter what either of you think?" The preacher becomes agitated by Mike's tone. Preacher Brent speaks with a stern voice. "Mike, that woman was my wife. And right now, you are not welcome. Elizabeth would not have liked you upsetting everyone. I have to ask you to leave, right now!"

Mike looks at him hard and tries to compose himself. "I'm sorry for her sake. But we have some business that is not finished. I will give you some time to grieve, but after that, things are going to change around here." Mike storms out. Doctor Madison replies. "I am so sorry. I really thought a lot of Ms. Elizabeth."

Mike walks off and jumps on his horse and in frustration calls out for Doc Madison. "Doc Madison!" The doctor realizes that Mike is very angry and. tries to hurry toward his horse. He turns to the preacher. He says, "I best be going." He walks out and gets on his horse and they both ride off.

With a coffin in tow, a wagon pulls up to the back of the church where tombstones are spread out and grassy land surrounds them. Many families are on wagons, and some are on horseback coming to pay their respects to the Carson family for their loss. There are so many wagons and horses lined up heading toward the church as Mrs. Elizabeth was a very well respected and loved person.

Everyone pulls up to the back of the church and the men get off and the undertaker entreats them to assist him with removing the coffin from the wagon. Some of the male church members help him place the coffin in the grave. Jonah, Joshua, Bill, Alice, Preacher Brent, and church members walk up and gather at the grave.

There is a sadness that can be felt all around as the sound of many crying fills the air. Jonah is overcome with grief and has tears flooding down his face. "What are we going to do without Ma?" Joshua replies, "I don't know Jonah. Ma would have wanted us to help Pa." Jonah replies.,"How can we help? I want Ma." He begins to cry even harder. Joshua grabs him and hugs him tight.

Alice begins to sing a song, and everyone becomes misty as they think of Elizabeth as Alice's voice rings out with the sound of pain in her voice. Preacher Brent reads a verse of the scripture and his voice sounds raspy from the pain of his loss and many tears shed. Mike McCray is in the distance, behind a cluster of trees watching the burial; he wipes a tear from his face sharply and walks off.

Five years later, a harder looking Mike McCray is sitting on the porch smoking a cigar. His cowhands are waiting for his instruction on dealing with the homesteaders who Mike calls outlanders. Johnny rides up on his horse from checking the fences on the McCray ranch. Mike calls out to his ranch hand, Johnny. "Johnny, good you are back. I want you to go by that healer, Negro's place and scare them into leaving this town."

Larcey looks up and speaks with confidence. 'Yeah, it's about time we did something." Mike replies, "I told them I was going to get them for what they have done to this town." He walks over to the window. Larcey looks over at his father and questions him. "Are you doing this because of the town or that preacher's wife?" He grabs Larcey about his collar hard and the intensity in Larcey's face shows that Mike hurt him. Mike jerks him closer to him as he speaks.

"Don't you worry about my motives! We going to just throw a scare into that Negro, so none of them wants to ever come round these parts again." Larcey replies, "Ok, sir. But I want to go too." Mike replies, "You'll get your chance soon enough. Johnny, take some of the boys with you. Do whatever you have to do."

115

The sound of horse's feet are hitting the ground. Men are riding into the night toward the Barnaby place, and they arrive at the farm when darkness has fallen and only the moon shine can be seen. Bill Barnaby is putting the horses up for the night and he hears a noise. Three men jump Bill from behind and pull him into the woods. They are pummeling him with punches; Bill gets a few hits in. Two of them grab Bill and hold him while the others keep hitting him.

Suddenly, there is a rustling sound and the neighing of the horse that startles the men. It is the preacher riding up and he hears a strange noise at Bill's house and starts to ride up fast. The men throw Bill down and quickly ride off. The preacher yells out. "Whose out there?" Bill is on the ground near some bushes in horrible pain. Bill is making sounds from the pain he is feeling from the beating. "Oh, ouch. mmm."

The preacher is trying to find Bill and calls out to him as he gets closer. "Is that you, Bill?" Bill replies, "Yeah. Oh, mmm." Bill grabs his stomach and the moonlight shines on Bill's face and it is a little beat up. Preacher Brent helps him to his feet. Mike, Johnny, and the men are sat out on the porch of the McCray ranch bragging about the raid on Bill Barnaby.

Johnny says, "That Barnaby was sure scared. I never seen a "darkee" so scared before. You think he cleared out?" Mike replies, "Did you beat him up bad?" Johnny replies, "He'll think twice about staying in this town. But something happened and we had to get going because someone was coming."

Mike stands to his feet in frustration and hits on the porch railing. "You mean you ran. Did you even see who it was?" Johnny replies, "I don't know, it looked like the preacher's horse." Mike replies, "You should have taken care of him too. That's okay. His time is coming."

THE ATTACK ON HOMESTEADERS

Three more years have passed at the McCray ranch. Mike and Johnny, and his ranch hand, are talking at the front door as Martha cooks breakfast. Martha serves Larcey as he sits at the table eating his breakfast while listening intently to Mike and Johnny's conversation. Johnny is reporting to Mike what the homesteaders have been doing. "Mr. McCray, they been putting stuff by the south fence again."

Mike slams his fist down hard on a chair in anger. "You know them outlanders are really pushing me! I told Preacher Brent I didn't want them near that fence at all." Mike looks out at his fence which seems to be miles-long as it stretches across his land filled with cattle. Whistles and pops can be heard as the cowhands wrangle the cattle to prepare them for transport.

Johnny replies. "Well, the preacher was down there earlier with a new family maybe named Johnson helping them till the land." Mike looks out and sees homesteaders in the distance working on a new home. " What! That's it. I have had it with that preacher. It's time to do something permanent to stop him for good. I mean it this time."

Larcey wants to impress his father by helping them get rid of the outlanders. "Pa, I heard you say you going do something about them outlanders and I want to go this time." Martha stirs a pot of porridge on the stove; she stops abruptly and walks quickly into the room.

"Now, Larcey you come on back over here and eat your vitals." As Mike turns to Martha, he pushes her out of the way with his hand. "Hush woman! "He turns to Larcey as he speaks. "You want to go out with the boys this time?" Larcey stops eating and looks up at his mother. "Yeah, Pa, put me in charge. I'll deal with em for yah." Mike replies, "You sure you got the stomach for this boy. I want the job done right, you understand?"Mike walks over to him and puts his hand on his shoulder. Larcey looks up at him smiling.

"I understand Pa." Johnny tells him, "We are going do it tonight then." Larcey stands up and pushes Johnny away. "I say when we do it!" Mike walks over to Larcey and looks down at him. "Calm down boy, Johnny was only trying to help ya. It's best to do it at night." Larcey shakes his head in agreement. "We can do at night when they are holding one of them church meetings.

That will put a scare into all them outlanders!" Mike pats Larcey on the head with a prideful smile. "I think the boy has a good idea. Yeah, do it when they are having the church meeting." Johnny gets a concerned look on his face. "But then, they might see who it is." Larcey turns around and has a big smirk on his face. "Y'all can wear a mask if you afraid of em."

Johnny stands firm and puts his hand on his gun. "I ain't afraid or nothing. I just thought." Larcey stands with confidence and walks over to Johnny. "We want them to know it's us. That will stop em from squatting on our land." Mike is watching the conversation as he interjects. "Yeah, you go ahead and do that boy. But you make sure you do it right, ya here." Larcey jumps to his feet and is hurrying to leave. "I won't let you down, Pa."

Martha jumps in between Larcey and Mike. "Mike, don't do this; they are peaceful folk. They ain't never did nothing to us. Plus, they ain't squatting, you know that!" Mike pushes her to the side, and she falls to the floor. "Move out the way woman. I told you about coming between me and my boy." Mrs. McCray looks up at him with fear as she speaks. "All this fighting is because of that dead woman who ain't never cared about you."

Mike raises his voice. "This ain't about her. You need to watch yourself." Martha points to Larcey as she speaks. "Don't make Larcey get into something that's between you and that preacher who never did anything to you but marry Elizabeth." Mike storms out of the house and slams the door behind him. Larcey runs over to his mother to try and help her up. "Ma, why you always trying to stir him up. She's gone. It's over."

As Martha is getting up from the floor, she looks seriously into Larcey's eyes. "It will never be over. He wants revenge and he won't stop until the same hate fills you that's in him." Larcey sits her down in a chair and straightens out her clothes. "Ma, I'll be alright. Just don't rile him again, please Ma."

Martha touches his face with care. "Okay son, but don't do this, please." Larcey tries to convince his mother that he has to do what his father wants. "I have to Ma. I must prove to him I'm strong like him. I want him to be proud of me." Martha holds his face in her hands as she speaks. "I'm proud of you, isn't that enough?" Larcey walks out to the porch where the men are gathered. Martha yells out, "Larcey! Larcey! No."

She sobs with despair. Johnny and Ben are on their horses anxious to ride out to crush some homesteaders. Larcey walks over and gets on his horse with a confident expression on his face as he climbs up into the saddle. Mike stands in support as he speaks to Larcey. "You ready, son?" Larcey sits up on his horse. "I'm ready. Let's ride." The men all start to ride out quickly as Mike watches them leave.

They ride across the open country and head toward a campfire service attended by the preacher and members of the church. When they arrive, the church members are singing a song with the preacher. When they finish singing, Preacher Brent begins orating a sermon. They are all praising the Lord and Preacher Brent Carson is standing in front of the members as they are clapping and praising the Lord exuberantly.

After the service, some of the church members decide to stay and listen to the preacher talk about the problems they are having with McCray. Preacher Brent says, "We are simple folk trying to learn what the Lord has for us. What better way to learn than through the Good Book? The Good Book says that if we plant our crop, we will reap what we sow. So, we planted a good crop this year." The people are shouting and clapping at the preacher's exciting speech.

The congregation says, "Yes, Lord! Amen." The preacher looks up and begins speaking. "The Good Book says that we should love our neighbors. Do the McCray's show us any love?" The congregation shouts. "No!!!" Preacher Brent continues talking. "But brothers and sisters, we must remain peaceful. We cannot let McCray rile us."

A strange look comes over Bill's face as he speaks. "But, last week one of the McCray men burned my barn. Where do I put my livestock now preacher? I say we fight back, or we will lose everything, our homes, and our land!" Alice Barnaby grabs her husband's arm as she speaks. "My husband is a peaceable man. He doesn't harm anyone. Most of you here know that. But we have a child to provide for, and we can't stand by and let McCray tear down everything we have."

The raging fire reflects the swirling and fiery emotions of the church members. In a firm voice, Carl answers, "Yes, Bill and his Missy are telling the truth. I had dealings with those McCray's, and they keep telling us that we are moving too close to their Land. This is free land!" The preacher walks over to settle Carl down as he talks. "Right! what do we care if they tell us we don't belong? This is God's country. We came here and staked our claim within the law."

Eric says, "Preacher, you know there ain't no law round these parts! You got to go clear to the soldier's camp in Ft. Johnson to get any help. And that's a three-day ride going and coming." The preacher looks over at Eric and holds up his Bible and pats the book. "We don't need no soldiers to help us keep our land if we got the Good Book, right!"

Joshua walks out and stands with his father and says, "Right! Amen preacher. No McCray is going kick us off our land." Preacher Brent says, "Look at that. My boy Joshua, he ain't afraid. You folks going to let a little boy shame you? What's the matter with all of you? Look over there at my younger boy, Jonah. I have my sons with me. Don't I, boys?" The people begin to look at each other and mumble their concerns.

Alice Barnaby looks around at the disgruntle faces and decides to support the preacher. "Well, maybe the preacher's right." Alice grabs Bill's hand and stares him down trying to get him to agree. Bill looks in the eyes of his wife and decides to back his friend. "Well, I guess we could try." Preacher Brent walks around the members with enthusiasm and shakes their hands as he speaks.

125

"Well alright! Come on, folks. If Brother Barnaby and Sister Barnaby can stay and be peaceable, we can all do it too. Are you with me?" The congregation shouts. "We're with you, preacher!" Preacher Brent starts charging the members up with positive orations. "So, will we let the McCray's steal our land?"

All the people shout. "No!" Preacher Brent tells all the members to speak out loud to the Lord. "Tell the Lord you mean to keep your land! Pray with me, brother. Pray with me, sister." The people tell him, "We're praying, preacher, we're praying." Gunmen riding horses unexpectedly surround them and terrorize them. All the people begin running fearfully in different directions while the men on horseback chase them like cattle.

One of the men grabs a flaming log and throws it on the roof of the preacher's barn and it begins to burn. People run everywhere as the barn burns in the background, with the cross crumbing into the roof. Men are riding on horses yelling, "Get out of here, you outlanders" as they shoot their guns. The men continue to go through the crowd of people throwing pots, food, bibles, and tables out of their way.

Preacher Brent says, "Now stops this! You men stop it! He tries to grab one of the men. Larcey McCray tells them, "You want us to stop? We'll stop preacher. We'll stop when you outlanders pack up and get!" Preacher Brent walks up to Larcey as he speaks. "We are not leaving. This is our land, and we mean to stay." Larcey McCray looks down at the preacher with disdain. "Look boys, the preacher says they mean to stay. Let's show em we don't take no guff from the likes of them." He throws the Bible down, and as it hits the ground, the preacher feels Larcey's disrespect.

As he is praying for God to help, a cowhand ties a rope around his feet. Two other cowboys hold him down as they put a rope on his feet and hook it up to a horse. The outlanders all stand around looking afraid with their wives and children. Alice Barnaby streams out anguish. "Preacher! No!" Preacher Brent says, "Now, I'm all right, don't nobody do nothing foolish now."

As the preacher is laying on the ground tied up, he looks at the members with the assurance that he will be okay. Jonah runs over and hits Larcey and he pushes Jonah down and holds him. Jonah's face shows horror and disappointment as he sees church people running scared.

He breaks loose and stands in the middle of all this terror. Joshua grabs Jonah and moves him out the way as the men are riding off. Hysterically, Jonah runs toward Larcey trying to help his father once again. Larcey McCray pushes Jonah down again and keeps on holding him down. Now you all be good, little outlanders, and nobody else will get hurt. Drag him, Ben! He slaps the horse's backside, and the horse takes off.

Ben laughs as he sees the cowboy drag the preacher. "Yee Ha!" Jonah says, "No! No! Not my Pa! You leave my Pa be." He strikes at the men with sticks and starts to hurl rocks at them. Jonah runs over again and starts hitting Larcey with his fist. Larcey pushes him down again and holds him as he squirms in anger. "Now your Pa wouldn't listen, so we just teaching him a lesson.

You hold still now. We're not hurting him much." Jonah keeps moving around trying to pull himself free as he shouts out. "No! Pa! Somebody, help him!" The men drag him until he appears near dead and then they ride off. The sun has gone down and it is dark. Jonah and Joshua are walking up the road; it is so dark it is difficult for them to see. Jonah stumbles on a rock in frustration and he starts yelling out to Joshua. "Joshua, what are we going do? Everybody is gone."

Joshua continues to walk. "It'll be alright. We just need to find Pa." Jonah panics, "He's dead, I know he is." Jonah starts to cry. Joshua looks at Jonah, "Stop it! We going to find him. We just need to get to Mr. Bill." As Jonah trudges through the darkness, "I can't see nothing." Joshua hears something, "Be quiet." Brent's body is bruised and hurt, and he makes a sound. "Ooaa."

Jonah and Joshua run quickly trying to find where the noise is coming from. "Did you hear that?" Jonah falls over him," No, ooaa." Brent in extreme pain, makes a painful noise. "Aww! Pa, Oh No!" Preacher Brent's body looks to have many injuries and as he tries to move, he makes sounds of pain. "Ooaa. Mmm" Joshua is trying to remain calm, "Quite it down. He can't move, he's hurt bad."

Jonah is horrified and afraid. "What are we going to do?" Jonah grabs his head like he is about to lose his mind. Joshua speaks in a strong voice. "Start gathering sticks. We need to make something to drag Pa on." Jonah tries to appear brave. "Ok. He starts to pick up things." Joshua is finishing up the contraption to drag Preacher Brent. Jonah questions, "You think that will hold him?"

Joshua says, "Yes, but we have to roll him onto it." They roll him onto the stick bed they made and begin to lift him. Preacher Brent's body is limp as it appears that it is all bruised and wounded. Ooaa,Ouch! Joshua feels bad that he is hurting him as he is trying to move him. "I'm sorry, Pa." Jonah looks at his father with concern. "He's hurt bad, Joshua." Joshua tries to reassure Jonah. "We just need to get him to Mr. Bill place. He'll take care of Pa."

Jonah looks at his brother with trust in his eyes. "How you know where it is. I can't see anything. I know it by heart; I can smell the herbs Mr. Bill grows." Jonah and Joshua are dragging the preacher on a bed of wood and leaves until they get to the road that leads to Bill Barnaby's farm. Jonah starts running up the road anxiously yelling in fear. "Ms. Alice! Ms. Alice! Where are you?"

The preacher is bloody and bruised from being dragged so far. Jonah reaches Alice's door and is knocking hard enough to break the door off the hinges. When she opens the door, she sees the preacher in his broken state and her face looks hurt and strained.

Alice is rushing trying to help Jonah with the preacher. "Oh boys, let me help you." She runs off the porch helping Joshua lift Preacher Brent by his arms into the house. Horror overcame Jonah as he looks at his father's mangled body. Mrs. Barnaby tends to Preacher Brent wounds. Jonah rushes through the house looking for Mr. Bill from room to room. "Where is Mr. Bill?" Alice sees that Jonah is alarmed. "He was out looking for Preacher Brent."

Joshua starts toward the door, stops and turns to Alice. "Where do you think he might be looking?" Jonah stands and looks at his father. "Will he be back soon?" Alice is working frantically to clean up the preacher's wounds. "Joshua, Joshua! Yes, Ma'am." Alice grabs more clothes trying to cover the cuts. "Your Pa is going to be all right. But his legs are hurt bad. I'm going to need you to go back to where we had the church meeting. See if Bill is around there still looking for the preacher."

Joshua pulls open the door. "Yes, Ma'am." Alice is putting clothes in the water and dressing the preacher's wounds, the water is red with his blood. "Get the horse from the barn and hurry!" Joshua replies. "Yesum." Alice sees Jonah looking at the blood-colored water.

"Jonah, Jonah! You come here and help me with your Pa while your brother goes to find Bill." Joshua rides off quick on his horse down the road as dust puffs trail after him. Jonah's face while his body trembles in fear, thinking of his father. "Yes Ma'am." Wiping tears from his face as his body is trembling in fear for his father.

Jonah takes a long look at his father's broken and fragile body. He cringes as he witnesses the pain that his father is in as Alice moves him and he yells out in agony. He realizes that Preacher Brent may die tonight. Alice encourages Jonah by squeezing his hand to help and not worry. "He's going to get better; it will just take some time." Jonah looks at his father's bruised legs. Will he walk again?" Alice looks up at Jonah's fretful face." I don't know, Jonah. I don't know."

Later that night, McCray is sitting in a chair on the porch of his ranch as he sees the cowboys ride up. "Did you do it?" Larcey climbs down off his horse and begins walking toward the porch. "We did it, Pa, but we didn't kill him." Mike McCray says, "I told you I want those outlanders run out of town, what's keeping you from doing the job?"

Joshua and Bill ride up quick, running up on the porch and go into the Barnaby house. Preacher Brent looks horrible as Bill takes care of him, his clothes are torn and ragged from being dragged. Alice attempts to clean Preacher Brent's wounds with some wet cloths. Bill tends to the cuts as she cleans them, working feverously to stop the loss of blood. Jonah and Joshua wait in the outer room looking defeated.

Two years later, an old Preacher Brent is sitting out on his worn-out porch in his wheelchair. Joshua brings the Bible and a blanket to cover his father in his wheelchair. "Do you need anything else Pa?" "No, I got everything I need right here, son." He gestures to his Bible in his lap. "Pa, you always stand by your principles. I admire you for that."

"A man can only stand on the things he believes. I believe in this Good Book." He holds up the Bible and shows it to his son. "Nothing else has been more faithful to me than this. For twenty years, I have followed the Lord and trusted him. He kept me on this path. I could not have done it on my own." Joshua leans against the post on the porch and looks at his father with unease.

"Do you ever feel like you should have done things differently though?" He looks over at his son and their eyes meet with deep-seated anguish. "You mean about what happened?" Joshua walks over and touches him on the shoulder. "Yeah, I think about what they did to you." Joshua piers down at his feet with an expression of irritation.

"I mean it angers me. I think how if it were me, I don't think I could feel like you about it." Preacher Brent rubs his Bible. "Joshua, a man hurts when harm is done to him. But hurting another man is not the answer."

Joshua hits his hand against the door of the house. The preacher observes Joshua's increasing anger as he recalls the trauma of that night. Joshua turns with a face full of confusion. "But what do you do with your pain though?"

REVENGE ISN'T SWEET

Two years later, Mike McCray watches the settlers are on an open range as the preacher holds a prayer meeting. He observes them on his horse with a disapproving scowl on his face while settlers build a new home in the distance. A proud Mike McCray stands with his hundreds of acres of land surrounded by cattle and livestock as he looks out at them.

Later that day, Mike heads back toward the barn and finds his son, Larcey brushing down some horses, as the sound of cattle rings through the air. Larcey starts chucking hay in the barn for the horses to eat. Mike is angry with Larcey because he did not kill the preacher. "I told you, you had to kill that preacher to stop those outlanders. Now they're stronger than ever with that preacher in that wheelchair." Larcey keeps chucking the hay. "But, Pa, I can't kill no preacher, that's bad luck. Plus, it will upset the settlers all around. That's why we just tried to throw a scare into him, and he almost died."

Mike says, Almost and dead are two different things." When Larcey looks at his father, he realizes that his father will never change. He is a very angry man who holds onto hatred and always wants revenge. Larcey stops brushing down the horses and walks toward the house. Mike follows behind him.

Larcey keeps walking and turns and tells Mike. "I can't kill no preacher. It might make the settlers fight back." Mike replies, "What's one preacher against thirty men? We have more hands and men with guns. And those settlers are peaceable folk. They don't carry guns. Now you go back out there and chase them away." While walking toward the ranch, Mike continues to yell at Larcey about the mistakes he made with the raid on the preacher.

Mike says, "I want you to catch them all together so that we can make our meaning plain, and kill that preacher, ya hear! Larcey says, How are we going to get them all together and give them a good whipping besides." Mike responds, "Boy, you don't know nothing, do ya? They have those church meetings near every night. I think they have one tonight. You go on over there and rough up some of those settlers and take care of that preacher for good."

Larcey replies, "But they'll be in church service." Mike McCray voice pushes Larcey back as he bellows in rage. "I don't care! Didn't you get them the last time when they were in church?" "Yeah, Pa, but it didn't sit right with me the last time. I don't want to go back. He can't even walk no more."

Larcey looks down at his shoes in shame, in disbelief at what his father is asking him to do. Mike tells him, "You do whatever you have to do to get rid of those lily-livered cowards! Now you ride on over there right now." Ben, Cody, Larcey and Johnny begin mounting their horses. Larcey looks at his father.

Larcey says, "Come on boys, saddle up and let's ride. We going to break up some outlanders tonight!" Ben says, "Yeah, let's ride." Cody says, "All right then, I can't wait to get em! Yeeha!" They ride off quickly into the open prairie toward the settler's homestead. They make a turn away from the settler's land and head toward town as Larcey has second thoughts about what Mike told him to do.

As Larcey and the McCray men ride to the saloon, the sound of singing and drinking wafts through the town. The men hitch up their horses and go in playing around and patting each other on the back. Ben goes over to the bar and looks around the room. "Your Pa ain't going to like the fact that we didn't throw a scare into them outlanders." Cody looks out of the side of his eye at Larcey. "Yeah, why didn't we do it, Larcey?" "How would I look running behind an old man, who can't even walk? I'm not doing it, no matter what Pa says."

Ben shakes his hand nervously as he takes a drink. "But your Pa will find out."Larcey slams his glass down and looks at his men. "Who's gonna tell em. You, Ben? You Cody?" Ben tells him, "No, I'm just saying." Larcey stands and looks at him with a coarse look. "Now, what Pa don't know won't hurt him." Larcey throws back a few drinks and taps on the bar for the bartender to give him another. Cody replies. "But he'll know if you killed him or not, won't he?"

Larcey looks at Cody in frustration and says, "Yeah, but I'm going to tell him that, the old man was near dead when I left him. That's what I'm going tell him, ya hear!" Ben gets a little fidgety in his seat thinking about what Mike may do to them if they mess up this job. Ben says anxiously, "Well, let's just ride over so we can say we was there. He won't know any more than that. But let's ride over anyway."

Larcey looks at Ben with a strange look and bangs his glass down for one more drink. Larcey says, "Maybe, you're right Ben. We'll ride over and throw a scare into him. But I ain't gonna kill him." Preacher Brent leads the church people in song and they are singing, standing, and clapping.

Preacher Brent begins singing another song titled, *'We're Getting Ready'*. The congregation looks on when abruptly men on horseback ride up shooting in the air. Larcey screams, "Preacher, you got to stop these people from settling on McCray land." "We ain't hurting nobody, we're settling and making our families here." Preacher Brent replies. We don't plan on leaving.

Larcey shouts, "Don't make me have to come back here and teach you another lesson, preacher."Despite being wheelchair-bound, the preacher still has bruises on his face from the McCray raid three years earlier. As Larcey makes another threat to hurt the preacher, all the church people watch. Jonah looks at them and starts yelling out. "What is wrong with you people? You gonna let them hurt an old man in a wheelchair? That's all you do is stand around and watch!"

Larcey laughs. "Looks like you got a problem preacher in your own house. Man's got trouble when his own kin don't look up to him." Larcey and his men ride off laughing, heading back to the McCray ranch.Preacher Brent replies. "Jonah, son, what were you doing? We don't want to start anything. I know how to handle this in a peaceful manner."

Jonah responds abruptly, "I can't do this anymore, Pa. I can't!" He runs off. Preacher Brent shouts, "Jonah! Jonah, you come back here, boy." Joshua shouts out. "Jonah, you hear Pa?" Jonah keeps going. Later that week, Joshua is in the Carson home tending to the preacher as Jonah comes into the house. Joshua says, "Where you been? Pa's been worried sick." Jonah responds, "Thinking." Joshua asks, "Thinking, Thinking about what? About how you embarrassed Pa?"

Jonah says, "I been thinking about how I don't fit in here." Joshua replies, "You're, just young. It'll be better when you get a little older." "It'll be better." Jonah yells, "You don't understand! I see what they did to Pa every night in my dreams. I wish I could kill Larcey McCray!" Joshua looks at him shocked.

He walks over to his brother trying to calm him. "You don't mean that."Jonah says, "All I know is the McCray's think Pa is a coward. They ain't gonna ever leave us alone." Joshua fumes as he defends his father to Jonah. "Pa ain't no coward. He's a brave man. You don't understand. He believes in turning the other cheek which is what the Good Book says.

141

It says love your neighbors…" Jonah cuts him off and yells, "Look at Pa! Can't you see our neighbors don't love us!" Joshua responds, "You will learn, little brother. You will learn." Jonah's eyes are filled with anger. "Learn what? Everyone thinks Pa is a coward. I can't go into town without hanging my face in shame. They all make fun of me, my Pa, and what happened." Joshua says, "Try to understand…" Jonah is frustrated and cuts him off again.

"I don't want to understand. Pa gives everything we have to the settlers. We keep working and the McCray's, they come along and tear it all up. I just want my share. I been working the farm since Ma died." Joshua looks at his brother in disbelief as he appears to be turning against his family.

Jonah responds, "I can't stay here because death surrounds us." Joshua replies, "I know you loved Ma. Pa loved her too." Jonah states, "Ma died because we couldn't afford a real doctor! Because Pa spent all our money to help them settlers. That's how she died. And he's still helping them, Joshua." Jonah pushes against Joshua heading towards the woods.

"I'm going to tell, him how I feel. I have to leave. I want to get away from this death and start living my life." Joshua yells out. "Wait, Jonah, you know, Mr. Bill is a good healer. No one could have done more. You know he did his best. Mr. Bill is a good man." Jonah turns around. "But he's not a doctor. I don't want to hear anymore!" Joshua says "Jonah! Jonah!" Jonah says, "Leave me alone!" He storms off, walking for miles and stumbles upon Matt Barnaby riding down the road.

Matt replies, "Hey, Jonah. What are you doing out here wandering around without a horse?" Jonah responds, "I don't know, just thinking. I just felt like walking." Matt asks, "Want me to give you a ride back?" Jonah says, "No, I'm going sit out here a while." Jonah leans against a rock looking up at the sky lost in thought as Matt dismounts his horse. Matt asks, "How bout if I join you?" Jonah throws his hands up in disgust and replies, "Suit yourself."

Matt asks, "How bout you tell me what's troubling you." Jonah says, "You wouldn't understand." Matt responds, "It's bout that raid ain't it?" Jonah abruptly states, "I just don't understand why my father always protects everyone except himself. I mean…" Matt cuts him off.

143

"You mean, you thought he should had fought back, and shot or killed one of them men. Jonah says, "Yeah, I felt that way too." Shocked Matt responds, "You know Jonah, I guess my folk have had to learn to fight without throwing a blow many times. Many a Negro been killed for fighting back and his family too."Jonah gets up and starts walking down the road.

Matt leads his horse after him. Jonah replies, "But least your folks fought back and weren't cowardly." Matt comes to a halt, looking at Jonah angrily. Matt replies, "So you think my father's a coward for keeping silent and not fighting the white man when they say things to him. Why? He'd be fighting half the world." Jonah replies, "Okay, maybe your situation is different. But things didn't have to be this way in my life." Matt asks, "Why, because you a white man and I'm a Negro? I'm a man and your father accepted my father as a man, and as a friend." Matt echoes the words of his father.

"He believes what the Good Book says. I mean he really believes we are all God's children, and he lives it." Jonah rages on, "He lets things go too far! None of the people at the church even tried to help him when the McCray's started in on him. None of them!"

Matt nods. "Well, you right to be angry. But, when you teach people to be non-violent, then they forget how to fight with their fists. I mean, Your father taught us not to do things like that. But turning the other cheek is hard for a man who ain't had to do it much in his life. My family has had to do it a lot."

Matt and Jonah rest for a moment from walking as Matt gives his horse a little water. Jonah is still upset about his father turning the other cheek and continues to rant to Matt about it. Jonah says, "Turning the other cheek! I'm so sick of hearing that. I been teased and harassed in town because they think I'm a coward like my father. Well, I'm not!" Matt shakes his head at Jonah. He can't believe Jonah cares so much about what other people think of him.

Matt replies, "You can't let other people sway your thinking. A man got to choose his road and stick to it."Jonah turns to Matt lowering his voice. "Sometimes a man has to make another road for himself. When the one he's on is too hard or mixed up crazy for him to live." A heaviness comes over Jonah's face. He replies, "I got to go Matt. I can't talk to you no more." Jonah hurries off into the woods.

145

Matt tries to catch him. "Wait Jonah, I can give you a ride."Jonah disappears into the woods. Matt rides up to the Barnaby farm and as he gets off his horse, he sees Bill brushing and watering the horses. "Glad you here, son. What took you so long? You know I need you to till this ground here."Matt walks by him, picks up his tools and begins to till the dirt quietly. Bill asks, "Matt, son you alright? You ain't had no trouble in town, have you?" He looks at him concerned wondering why Matt is so quiet.

Matt turns to his father and says, "No. I just been talking to Jonah." Bill asks, "Jonah? Where did you run into him?" Matt responds," He was walking up the road and I just stopped and talked to him. He seemed upset, *real* upset."Bill asks, "About what?" Matt replies, "He blames us for what happened to the preacher. Us? I don't mean just us, but everyone for not fighting back when the McCray men attacked us."

Bill says, "Well, you know it's hard for Jonah. He lost his Ma and now the preachers in a bad shape." Bill walks over to Matt and begins helping him till the land. Matt says, "He thinks we're all cowards, Pa." Bill drops his hoe turning to Matt and replies, "Well, son, now, you know we're not cowards.

146

You learned a long time ago that there's many ways to fight back in this world." Matt puts down his hoe and looks at his father with respect. Matt replies, "I know Pa, but I think Jonah is heading down a destructive road. He just seemed so lost and troubled. I have you and Ma, but he feels so alone."

Bill puts his arm around his son. "He has his father. I know Preacher Brent can get caught up sometimes with helping folks, but he loves those boys."

THE PRODIGAL SON

Three days later, Jonah comes into the house looking for his father. Joshua tries to refrain him because he knows Jonah will upset his father. Jonah moves Joshua out of the way and says, "Pa, I need to talk to you about some things." Joshua walks in front of Jonah and puts his hand on Jonah's chest and says, "Jonah, don't!" Preacher Brent is sitting in his wheelchair looking confused about his son's tussling in front of him.

Preacher Brent says, "Now, quit this you are brothers. So, you decided to come home, did ya boy?" Jonah says, "Yes, sir. Pa, I'm home, but not for long." Preacher Brent says, "What's on your mind, boy. You seem to be troubled." Jonah looks down and back up at his father and says, "I am troubled, Pa." Preacher Brent says, "What's troubling you?" Jonah replies, "Pa, I don't feel like a member of this family any longer. Since Mom passed away, I don't feel like I belong here anymore."

Preacher Brent says, "What's your meaning, boy?" Jonah looks him in the eye. "I don't believe the same things you and Joshua do." Preacher Brent responds, "Your Mom believed, and you been believing all these years. Now what done changed your mind bout God?" Jonah walks away and turns and looks at all the pictures of his family from when he was younger.

He sees one of him and his Mom together and his heart burns with anger. He turns around and says, "It's not God, Pa. It's you." Preacher Brent looks at Jonah bewildered with a shocked expression on his face. "Me. I don't understand what you mean." Jonah responds, "I just don't want to end up like you. Look at you! You work and work, and what do you have to show for it?" Preacher Brent grabs his Bible and holds it firmly. "The good Lord has my riches, boy. I am working for Him."

Jonah says, "But Pa, you give everything to all the church folk. If this keeps up, it won't be nothing left for Joshua and me." The preacher puts his Bible on the table and looks at Jonah with a displeased expression. "So that's it. Is that what you worrying about boy? Some money? Joshua! Joshua!" Preacher Brent coughs a little because he is very upset with Jonah. Joshua hurries over trying to assist his father. "Yeah, Pa, what's wrong?"

Preacher Brent points to a cabinet where he keeps his money. He tells Joshua, "Go over and get that satchel for me." Joshua walks over and picks up a satchel and gives it to his father. Preacher Brent throws it to Jonah abruptly as if he does not care about the money inside the satchel. The preacher says, "Here boy, take that! Take it and see what you can do to make you happy."

Joshua gets a look of concern on his face as he does not believe his father is giving Jonah every bit of money they have in the world. "Pa! What are you doing?" Preacher Bent looks at Jonah with disdain. "Your brother wants his share of the farm. He says I'm squandering it all away on God's people." Jonah picks up the satchel and walks outside to put the money in his saddle, leaving the door open.

Preacher Brent stares for a moment at Jonah as he thinks about the boy. Jonah used to be reading the Bible with him in the parlor. Jonah looks back at the Preacher and his mind wanders into a daydream about the days he spent reading the Bible with his father. As Jonah mounts his horse, he is still caught in a daydream state. He sees himself as a child asking his father a question.

Jonah is remembering himself as a little boy sitting up under Preacher Brent telling him a Bible story. Jonah says, "Pa, why do you like the prodigal son story so much?" Preacher Brent says, "I guess because he comes home son and realizes that he should have never left." Jonah smiles as he is reading the story with Preacher Brent. Jonah asks, "But why did he leave in the first place."

Preacher Brent replies, "Because he wanted to find his own way in the world. But the world is a hard place without the love of your family." Jonah looks into the Preacher's eyes and responds, "I'm glad I have you, Pa." Jonah hugs his father and Preacher Brent hugs him back. The horse moves and neighs and Jonah snaps back into reality. He realizes it is only a daydream.

One year later, on Carson's farm, Joshua is working with Matt while Bill is helping them clear land for planting. Matt is pushing a lot of dirt in a barrel and dumps it in a pile nearby. Matt says, "You hear talk about what Jonah been doing these days? Joshua is walking up, hoeing and dropping seeds in as it is planting season.

Joshua says, "Yeah, he's in town running with the cowboys while I'm working on the farm." Matt stops and wipes some dirt off his hands as he goes back to pick up some stray rocks from the ground. Matt replies, "You sound a little upset." Joshua hesitates to speak but then says, "More like disappointed. I don't understand why my father let Jonah take the money and run off into town."

Matt grabs a hoe and starts helping Joshua with clearing and planting seeds. Matt responds, "Your Pa just wanted Jonah to see the difference, I suspect." Joshua turns around and looks Matt dead in the eyes with a serious face. "What's the difference? All he does is run around, drinking, and shooting things up with them outlaw cowboys from McCray's. I can't believe he is dealing with that man after everything that happened." Matt shrugs his shoulders. "Jonah is green and naïve, he doesn't know anything about those things. He's scared, I think."

Joshua replies, "Scared of what? He's going around with the people who have terrorized us." Matt sees that Joshua is hurting and walks over toward him, puts his hand on his shoulder. "I know you are disappointed in your brother. But I talked to Jonah before he left. He was real messed up about everything." Joshua drops the hoe to the ground and looks up at the sky and says," I hurt too, but I didn't run away."

Joshua and Matt walk over to the barn and sit down to rest a moment as they watch some chickens run around the yard. Matt turns to Joshua and says, "I know you do. But don't you remember what your mother's death did to Jonah?" Joshua slumps over in defeat with teary eyes.

Joshua states, "She was my mother too. I miss her just as much as he does." Matt puts his arm around him and responds, "Jonah not strong like you and I. Look at what happened to him when your father got hurt." Joshua looks Matt in the eye and says, "You sound just like my mother. She always thought that way about him. That's why she babied him so." Matt says, "She loved him; I'm sure she didn't mean to baby him. But the shock of what happened to the preacher really messed him up."

Joshua stands in frustration. "Then why is he running off and leaving my father like this now?" Matt gets up and starts toward the hay pile and begins chunking hay in the horse stall. He watches the horses eating. "He's hurting and trying to find his way." Joshua walks over and rubs on the horse's head.

"What do you expect me to do about it. I have to keep this place together. I don't have time to run after him." Matt says," Take care of your father and the farm. Jonah will come around." Taking a step towards the barn door, Joshua looks up to the sky with a determined face. "I don't have time to worry about that. He's in God's hands now."

Matt walks up behind Joshua and moves him forward to motion for him to step aside as he closes the barn door. Joshua walks with Matt as he says, "That's a good place for him then. We will let God handle the matter then. A man has to find himself sometime in life."

Joshua sees Jonah laughing with some cowboys a few months later while working on his father's farm. From a distance, he is able to hear them riding by.

RIOTOUS LIVING

A few months later, Jonah and some cowboys watched the dance hall girls dancing and drinking in the saloon. The owner of the prominent saloon in Red Springs looks at Jonah while she is talking to one of her dancehall girls about how handsome Jonah looks as he speaks to the other cowboys. Marybelle says, "I see you eyeing that Carson boy, May. Isn't he a little young for you?" The saloon is filled with noise as the cowboys are all at the bar drinking and jarring with each other.

The piano player is playing music. Some cowboys are at tables talking to saloon girls. May says, "when they come in here, they're fair game." Mary bell replies, "Does that mean I can go over?" May reaches over and grabs Marybelle's hand and says, "You do, and you'll have to deal with me." Marybelle pulls her hand back from May as she looks at her seriously.

Marybelle replies, "Okay. Okay. You saw him first. Just remember, he's that preacher's son." May get a look of surprise on her face. "What!" Sharing the juicy news and hoping to discourage May from approaching Jonah, Marybelle says, "Yeah, the preacher that the McCray boys nearly killed a while back."

May has a look of shock on her face, but it quickly turns to determination. "Well, it seems he's not as interested in preaching as he was, or else he wouldn't hang with McCray's men." Marybelle replies, "Go easy, May." May says, "I will." May walks over to the bar behind Jonah and whispers in his ear, "Buy me a drink?" He looks around with a curious expression on his face. "You talking to me?".

May moves closer and puts her hand on his chest. "Yeah, I'm talking to you." Jonah says, "Okay, Barkeep, set em up." May looks Jonah up and down suspiciously. "Aren't you a little young to be drinking?" Standing firm and placing his hand on the bar, Jonah leans back and smiles. "I'm older than I look.". As May drinks from her glass and looks over the brim, she says, "I bet you are."

She takes her hand and rubs it up and down Jonah's arm as she speaks with him. Jonah nearly tumbles over the spittoon and spills it all over the floor as he jumps back quickly. Ben, one of the McCray cowhands, is sitting at a table not far from the bar watching Jonah and May talk. In a jealous mood, Ben shuffles the cards while he calls Jonah to join him. "Jonah, come on over! Let's get the game started."

With her blonde hair and blue eyes. May makes Jonah feel almost as if she is hypnotizing him. Ben startles Jonah out of the hypnotic state of May when he calls out to him. "Okay, I'll be right over." Jonah turns around to May and tells her. "I'm sorry, we've got a game to play." May hides her irritation at Ben's interruption. "So, you're a gambling man." Jonah smiles and tilts his head back in a proud manner. "Yes, Ma'am, I am."May gets an angry look on her face as if she feels insulted.

She blurts, "Don't call me Ma'am, honey. I ain't old." The upbringing of his father to respect ladies comes across in Jonah's tone. May takes it to mean he is calling her old. While he moves back and takes a long look at her in her beautiful form-fitting dress, he thinks she is an attractive woman. But one who is a little older than him.

As he is unsure of what to say, he stumbles over his words. "What should I call you; that is, what is your name?" She rubs her hand across Jonah's face. "My name is May." The cowboys are sitting at the tables drinking and talking while they await May to perform. The Barkeep lets her know that she needs to go up to sing, he says, "You're Up, May. "

May says, "I'm sorry, I have to sing now. Will I see you after your game?" Jonah says, "Yes, Ma'am! I mean May." Joshua is loading his horse with sacks in front of the general store when he sees Jonah leave the saloon with McCray's men. As McCray's men ride toward the McCray ranch, Jonah and Ben are far behind. The horses of the men can be heard trotting quickly in the distance. As Jonah rides up next to Ben, he turns to him and says, "I've lost all my money, Ben. What am going to do?"

Ben pulls back on the reins of his horse. Ben replies, "Don't you worry, you're one of us now. Come on, I'll get you a job." Jonah states, "A job doing what?" Ben says, "Don't worry about that; I'll take care of you, my friend." In the ranch house, Jonah is sleeping. Jonah is lying in bed and begins to turn and twist as he appears to be dreaming. In his dream, men on horseback ride through the crowd and fire their guns.

He sees the church people running all over in his dream. The men on horseback chase the church members, and Jonah's body tightens. He sees one of the men throw a log from the fire into the preacher's barn in the dream.

He begins to sweat as he sees the barn on fire and everyone frantically trying to put it out.

The fire from the barn comes closer and closer until Jonah feels its heat. Turning, he throws the cover to the floor. He watches the cross burn and the smoke of the fire consume it. He sees the preacher walks up and tells McCray's men, "Now stop this! You men stop it!" In his dream, Jonah tries to grab one of the men and is thrown down.

The voice of Larcey rings in Jonah's head saying, "You want us to stop. We'll stop preacher when you outlanders pack up and get!" Jonah sees the Preacher tell Larcey, "we are not leaving. This is our land, and we mean to stay." Soon, Jonah sees the men get a rope out and one of the cowboys runs over and grabs his father while two other cowboys hold him down as they put a rope on his feet and hook them up to a horse.

Jonah sees the church members just standing around doing nothing, scared and afraid to help his father. Jonah keeps tossing, turning, and sweating with a look of fright on his face. Jonah violently awakened by his own voice as he hears himself say "No! No! Pa!" Jonah awakens abruptly. Jonah has a look of fear on his face as he awakens from the dream. Jonah gets up and cleans up and heads to the saloon.

When Jonah arrives at the saloon, he begins playing cards with May, and the saloon owner as other men are talking to saloon girls and making merry. A few cowboys are at the tables playing cards while others are just sitting having a drink and talking. Jonah and May decide to head over to the bar and Jonah swats May on the backside.

Jonah says, "Come here, girl!" May responds, "You're bad, boy. Nobody would ever know that you were a good boy once." Jonah smiles and grabs his drink and throws it down his throat. Jonah replies, "Now, don't you go bringing up the things of the past!" May laughs and grabs her drink and throws it back.

She taps on the bar with her glass for another. May responds, "Jonah, you know McCray has been looking for you." Jonah replies, "I'll see him soon enough. You just bring me a drink and sit yourself down right here." Dance hall girls are sashaying around and keeping the cowboys company. May responds, "I got to sing and dance in a minute." Jonah grabs her again and sits her down at a table. "You got time. Come on and keep me company for a minute."

Jonah motions to the barkeep to bring over some more drinks. May replies, "Well okay, just for a minute!" She laughs and gets up, sits in Jonah's lap, hugs, and hangs on to him. Ben walks up to the bar and says, "Barkeep!" The barkeeper turns around from serving drinks to the other cowboys. Then he begins cleaning up some glasses and wiping behind the bar. The barkeeper seems busy as he is moving some barrels aside to put some bottles on a shelf. Ben keeps rapping on the bar impatiently.

The barkeeper tells him, "I'll be right there, Ben!" Ben says, "Come on now, I'm parched!" The Barkeeper comes over and says, "What will you have?" Ben replies, "Took you long enough! I'll have a whisky." Ben throws it back and says," Ah set it up again." Ben keeps drinking and appears a little tipsy as he walks over to Jonah at the end of the bar drinking too.

Ben says, "Jonah, you know old man McCray been looking for you?" Jonah puts down his glass. "I'm going after this last drink." Ben smacks him on the back and says, He's pretty riled up. "You better hurry up!" Jonah looks at him with an annoyed face and tells him, "Okay, Okay! You wait for me now, May, I'll be back." Ben responds, "May don't have to wait. I'll keep her company."

He grabs May by the waist and pulls her close, stumbling a little. May is bothered by Ben touching her in this way and tussles with him. She tells him, "You get off me, Ben! Now go on." Jonah turns and see's what Ben is doing and May's reaction. He notices she is okay and he continues to walk out to get on his horse. As Jonah rides up to the McCray ranch, he sees the men working in the barn and horses moving around in the fenced area.

Mr. McCray walks out of the ranch house as Jonah is tying down his horse to the hitching post. Mike says, "Where you been?" Jonah replies, "In town at the saloon with May." Mike gets a funny look on his face and laughs. "Why you spend all your time with that gal? You know she ain't no good no how." Jonah walks up on the porch and sits down firmly and looks at Mike sternly. "Don't talk about May that way. She has a good heart."

Mike laughs and puts his boot up on the porch step and lights a cigar. A cloud of smoke fills the air as he is drawing in big puffs and blowing out smoke. Mike responds, "You sound like you Pa. A good heart. You are going soft on me boy?" Mike walks over close to Jonah and looks at him in the eyes. Jonah stumbles with his answer.

He is somewhat embarrassed that he does not tell Mike how he really feels about May. "No, I'm just saying May is just for hanging around. Weren't nothing serious." Mike slaps him on the back with pride and keeps smoking his cigar. "Good. A man has to pick a good clean woman when he thinks bout settling down." Jonah looks at him for the first time and sees what kind of man Mike really is when it comes to women.

He realizes that Mike only cares about himself. It makes Jonah feel a little troubled as he tries to cover it up. He blurts out trying to please Mike, "Who said anything about settling? I just enjoy her company is all." Mike seems pleased that Jonah isn't serious about May. Mike replies, "All right boy! You got the right idea. Have all the fun you can while you can. The time comes soon enough when a man has to make a choice."

Hearing Mike speak about May in this way begins to sicken Jonah. He becomes a little agitated. "Why did you send for me, Mr. McCray? Something wrong?" Mike responds, "Yes, I want you to go out to the open country and put a scare into some new settlers. And let them know how we do things around here." Jonah replies, "Yeah, I know how we do things around here."

Mike replies, "You know Jonah, I look at you like one of my own kin. I think you are just like me when I was young." Jonah gets a strange look on his face. "What makes you say that?" Mike responds, "Well, we both don't have no heart at all, do we? Ha-ha, Ha ha!" He hits him on the back.

Jonah's heart sinks as he thinks about his relationship with his father for a moment. Jonah says, "Yeah, no heart at all. What's it get you anyway?" Jonah starts walking toward the men who are now working on clearing some brush in the distance. Mike says, "See, that's what I mean. We are two of a kind. We don't need nobody. All we want is what we can have for ourselves and our kin."

Jonah looks at Mike and feels despair in his heart. He tells Mike, "Yes sir, you're right. We are two of a kind. Let me get Ben and Larcey so we can ride on out there." Mike's eyes fill with pride as he sees Jonah as the son he could have had with Elizabeth. Mike replies, "Yeah, boy, you go head." Mike calls out, "Ben, Larcey, you go on out there with Jonah. He going to throw a scare into some new settlers."

Ben replies, "Yeah, let's ride." Larcey walks over to Mike frustrated. "Pa, I told you I can handle them by myself. I don't need Jonah and Ben." Jonah puts his arm around Larcey's shoulder, trying to calm him. Jonah replies, "Aww, come on, Larcey let us tag along. Chasing outlanders is fun! You want to keep all the fun to yourself?" In a long glance at Jonah, Larcey wonders if he is serious before giving in. However, he is still suspicious of him. "Jonah, you're a strange man, but I like you! Let's go." The men mount their horses and ride quickly out of the corral.

THE PRICE OF FORGIVENESS

Matt and Bill are clearing and moving the hay to the barn so they can load it up in the hayloft. Alice brings out some water and scoops some out for Matt and Bill to drink. Some of the hay bales are tossed into the barn by Bill as he talks with Matt. Alice walks over to Bill and replies, "Did you get the supplies from town?" Bill responds, "No, I'll go in later and pick everything up."

Matt Barnaby replies, "I can go and pick up everything if you want me to, Pa." Bill says, "No, I want to go and drop some things off at Preacher Brent's home." Bill has not been to see the preacher in a couple of weeks because it is harvest time. He and his family have been working hard to get their crops pulled in. Matt replies, "How's he doing, Pa? I know it's hard for him all alone in that broken down old farm." Bill responds, "Well, he's doing as well as can be expected considering his condition and he has Joshua helping him.

I would have gone by, but we had all these crops to get done." Matt responds, "Why did that happen to him?" Bill replies, "It was a long time ago son, and a lot of folk round here don't like too much talk about it." Matt says, "I know most of it. I just don't understand why people would want to hurt someone like Preacher Brent."

Bill looks at him and puts his hand on his shoulder. He says, "Some people don't have a bit of kindness in them, just anger. That's why." Matt replies, "That is a sad shame. But why they call us outlanders? That don't make a bit of sense to me." Bill responds, "Alright! Alright, son, you know the town folks call us outlanders because we settled here from another place."

Matt responds, "But we are church people, and we believe in God. We're not outlanders even if we moved here from somewhere else. They don't want us because that don't make no sense at all." Matt sits down on a nearby stool and looks up at his father. Bill says, "Folk don't like anything different. They like things to stay the same." Matt is thinking about what Jonah said about his father being a coward for not standing up to McCray's men. He wants Bill to tell him why he let the men beat up on him.

Matt responds, "So, for all these years you have stopped them from hurting anyone by being a coward." Bill replies, "We're not cowards. We are peaceful people. That's what Preacher Brent taught us." Bill turns around quickly as he hears someone coming up to his farm. Bill says, "What! What's that? I hear horses and they are coming up fast. You take your Ma and go up in the loft in the barn."

171

Bill pushes Matt up the road toward the house. Matt responds, "Huh? Why?" Matt is confused and Bill pushes him harder. Bill responds, "Do it. Do it now boy!" Alice says, "Listen to your Pa. Hurry." Matt runs up to the house with Alice and the men ride up fast on Bill. Bill hurries over and grabs a shovel to defend himself then he sees a familiar face and puts his weapon down.

Bill replies, "Jonah, what are you doing here? How can you do this to us?" Bill gets a shocked look on his face which turns to disappointment. Jonah says, "I'm doing what needs doing after you stood around and let my Pa almost die. I was only a boy and the only one fighting for my Pa. You just stood there! You didn't do anything to help him. You cowards!" Bill goes to grab Jonah and Jonah snatches away from him with anger.

Bill responds, "Jonah, wait. Let me tell ya. You don't understand." Jonah pushes him off him. Jonah says, "You get off me! Now old man McCray told you to stop moving in on the north fence and you outlanders keep on settling." Bill looks at Jonah disapprovingly. "But he doesn't own that land. That's free territory." Jonah replies, "It's McCray land! McCray cattle graze there and been grazing there for as long as I can remember."

Bill stares in confusion at Jonah. "Since long as you can remember. What are you talking about? Don't you remember what they did to your Pa?" Jonah is furious with Bill and doesn't care what happens. He believes that Bill Barnaby and the members of the church are to blame for what happened to his father. Jonah's voice cracks in pain as he begins to describe the horror of the day his father was crippled and left for dead.

Jonah says, "I remember a lot of things. I remember all you outlanders being cowards! Now because of you, Pa can hardly move or do anything at all. I remember Pa's mangled body and I swore then and there that I wasn't gonna be a coward! Never! Burn it down boys! Burn it all down." Larcey rides up and looks Bill in the face and laughs.

Larcey replies, "Yeah, burn it! Ha, ha. That will teach 'em. Filthy outlanders." Bill is held down and laughed at by the men. Bill says, "No! You used to be one of us, too, Jonah! You used to love God. Read the Good Book with all of us. We never meant for your Pa to be hurt. We loved him." Jonah is trembling with anger and shouts out to Bill. "Shut up! I hate you, all of you. I will never be a coward like my Pa! I will never be a coward.

Look at what it did to him. He can't walk, ride or anything! Shut him up, Ben." Ben hits Bill hard enough to knock him to the ground. Ben responds, "Yeah, shut up. You heard him. You outlanders are like dirt to us." Jonah replies, "Come on, boys, let's ride. I feel like going into town and to see May." Jonah jumps on his horse and looks back at the barn that is now in flames.

Larcey says, "Yeah! I told you Jonah, you're a strange man. But I like how you think. Let's go boys." Ben gets excited and shouts. "Well alright! Yeeha! Horse make tracks." Despite his best efforts, Bill is unable to put out the fire in the barn. Alice and Mat rush out of the house, trying to put out the fire. Alice says, "Oh no!" She rushes over to Bill and tries to stop him from hurting himself because he has some cuts on his face.

Alice tries to sit Bill down. He keeps running with buckets of water trying to put out the fire. Finally, Alice gets him to accept that the fire will burn out and they will rebuild. Matt is enraged and can't believe Jonah did this to his family. The men are riding quickly through the prairie toward the saloon. The saloon is filled with people drinking and the dance hall girls are dancing in the background.

When the men burst into the saloon, Jonah goes to the bar and asks for a drink for the men. Jonah replies, "Set em up, barkeep!" Ben responds, "Yeah! All around." Larcey says, "One more right here! May says, what you boys been up to tonight?" Larcey responds, "We been running settlers out of town." Ben says, "Yeah! The best time I had in a long time." May replies, "What! Why you bothering them peaceful folk? They don't bother us no more.

They don't even come into town too much at all." Jonah replies, "Old man McCray said they been moving in on the north fence on his land. So, we had to teach them outlanders a lesson." May responds, "A lesson?" May grabs Jonah and pulls him to the side as she can't believe what he has just done." She responds, "Did you forget about the lesson they gave you and your Pa, ten years ago?"

Jonah replies, "May, I told you never to speak of that. That's past." She puts her hands on her hips and stares Jonah in the face with concern. May responds, "Jonah you don't even go and see your Pa. Do you know he's living in an old shack of a farm laid up in that bed? Don't you care at all?" Jonah says, "I can't help what happened to my Pa.

175

He has my brother there to take care of him anyway. I can't bear to see him like that. It ain't my fault he was a coward. That's why he's in that condition." Jonah says, "What's happening to you? Since when did you like outlanders?" May can't believe her ears and fastens her eyes on Jonah and a look of shame comes over her face. She quickly catches herself as the saloon is full of people.

May replies, "I never said I liked any outlanders! I just don't think it's right for you to leave your Pa in that house to die." Jonah with resentment turns to her and says, "He's fine. The church members take care of him. Those church folks, that he loved more than me. My Pa loves them and that Good Book!" He runs out of the saloon and rides away on his horse toward the open prairie.

The McCray Farm consists of hundreds of acres with fields that stretch for hundreds of miles. It is one of the best ranches in the territory, and it has fences that surround some of the most stunning horses. Mike's prime cattle fill up another fenced area of his land. While the sounds of cows, chickens, and pigs honk in the air on the other side of his ranch. Jonah rides up fast and throws his reins over the fence.

It's dark and Mike is out near the corral with the horses checking things before coming in. Mike hears a noise and grabs his lantern and waves it around. Mike replies, "Who's out there? Jonah says, It's me! Jonah." Jonah dismounted and started walking toward him in the barn. While he is working with the horses, he grabs the tackles and saddles and stores them away. Mike says, did you get those outlanders! Jonah starts rubbing the horse that keeps nudging him and reaches for some feed to put in his hand.

The horses feed from Jonah's hand as he says, "Yes sir, we burned down their farm. That should send a message to all them!" Mike looked at Jonah curiously out-of-the-corner of his eye and said, "Good job, boy. You ain't no outlander, not by far." As Jonah approaches Mike, he looks him in the eye and asks, "Why did you say that?"

Mike shakes his head and shrugs his shoulders as he says, "You know, Larcey's been talking. Saying that folks are talking about things that happened round these parts years ago. He thought maybe it bothered you. It was your Pa." Jonah says, "No, aint nothing bothering me."

Jonah snatches his hat off his head and shouts, "I ain't no coward!" Mike is surprised by Jonah's display of emotion but responds with excitement and joy. "That's my boy! I knew you were okay. It was just the boys had been talking." Jonah replies, "You don't have nothing to worry about. I ain't no Bible totting church member. Thinking that God can solve all my problems. No, I ain't." As Jonah walks towards his horse, his expression shows that he is very hurt and concerned about what he said to Mike.

As the night continues, Jonah is left with only the stars to guide him through the prairie. While Jonah is thinking out loud to himself, he hears some noise in the background. Jonah says. "That old man will be all right. Man doesn't have to be like his Pa. Man can't choose who's his Pa is anyway." When he hears singing, he slows his horse and gets down to see what is going on.

They are praising and worshipping God as they sing a song titled "We Are Marching to the Kingdom." around a fire. Then Jonah bursts in and starts screaming and shouting. "What are you singing? Jesus ain't your protector! You stupid outlanders. You are all going to die someday if you keep believing that."

Bill moves over toward Jonah and tries to calm him by extending his hand to Jonah's shoulder. Bill replies, "Jonah, you are hurting. We believe Jesus is our protector. The Good Book says so. You used to believe the same thing. Jonah pushes Bill away hard. "What are you doing here? Aren't you leaving town? You have nothing left.

We burned it all to the ground! As the church members look on, Alice stands with a look of disappointment on her face as she steps toward Jonah. "Red Springs is our home, and we aren't leaving. We forgive you, Jonah. We know you are trying to find your way." Churchgoers stare at Jonah in a disturbing manner as he throws his arms in the air and walks back and forth in frustration as he yells out.

"You people are crazy, weak cowards!" Matt gets aggravated by Jonah's display of disrespect and jumps in Jonah's face. "We're not cowards. It takes a strong person to forgive. It's easy to fight and hurt people." Jonah says, "You're crazy! You're crazy!"

OUT OF CONTROL

Jonah is disturbed by everything that happened during the church meeting and he bolts out into the night and hops on his horse and rides off erratically. The moonlight is dim, and Jonah comes through the bushes sitting on his horse near his father's farm. While he approaches the house, he sees his father reading on the porch in his wheelchair. Preacher Brent replies, "Who that be? Is someone out there? Show yourself I can't come to you."

When Jonah hears his father's voice, he gets off his horse and walks through the trees until he's on the porch. Jonah responds, "It's me Pa." Preacher Brent is sitting with a blanket covering his legs and a lighted lantern reading his Bible. Upon seeing that it is Jonah, the preacher's face lights up with joy at seeing his son. Preacher Brent responds, "Jonah, my boy, I've been praying for you to come." J

onah speaks sarcastically. Jonah says, "Yeah Pa, praying." Preacher Brent realizes that Jonah has not changed his way of thinking and it disturbs him to his core. In a displeased voice, the preacher replies, "You still don't believe. Do you boy?" Jonah looks down on his father and asks with disdain, "Believe what? That God is the answer to all my problems! No, I don't believe that."

Preacher Brent says, "You have to believe boy, you hear me!" Jonah bends down and gets in his father's face with his arms failing in his father's face. "Why! Why do I have to believe? Those church members left you for dead. They didn't even stop them from hurting you." Preacher Brent feels ashamed and broken as he talks to his son realizing that Jonah is full of anger.

He can't believe how Jonah feels about the people he helped over the years. He looks at Jonah and speaks in a hurt tone. "Them. Who is them, Jonah? Are they the people you are working for?" Jonah is all worked up and fully involved in the argument as he keeps getting in the preacher's face. Jonah says, "Yes, I work for McCray! They own everything for miles around. Yes, I do his dirty work. It's better than being a coward."

The preacher gets a look of defeat on his face as he realizes Jonah doesn't understand what God has blessed him to achieve all his life. The words of his son are like knives stabbing him in his chest, causing his heart to be torn apart. Preacher Brent says, "You think I'm a coward, son. You're the coward. A coward bullies people who are weaker than them.

182

That's a coward, not a person who is willing to stand and take whatever they have to for what they believe in. Don't you remember the story of Abraham?" Jonah is infuriated and turns away from his father and tosses his arms up with annoyance. Jonah replies, "I don't want to talk about it."

The preacher is disturbed and troubled to the point of being vexed by the harsh words of his son and he cuts him off. Preacher Brent responds, "Was he a coward for following God's instruction to make a sacrifice of his son Isaac? Then God provided the sacrifice; Abraham was considered favorable in God's eyes. Then all the generations of Abraham were blessed." Jonah continues to rant and yell at his father in an aggravated manner not realizing how he is upsetting the preacher.

He gets in his father's face with an infuriated look and then turns and starts walking off the porch. Jonah replies, "How do you believe in that stuff after all that happened to you. Why didn't you fight back?" There are people in the Bible who fought back!" Preacher Brent's face begins to turn red, and he is coughing as he is talking to his son. He begins to sweat and look ill, but Jonah doesn't notice.

The preacher continues shouting his proclamation of devotion to the Lord and why he has lived the life of ministry. The more the preacher raises his voice, the more he coughs. Preacher Brent responds, "Yes, but they were led by God to fight! There are many ways to fight son. Many ways. Ours is a peaceable one. Oh!" Suddenly, the preacher grabs his chest, and the words cease coming out as he is coughing and trying to catch his breath. Jonah's back is turned and he continues to talk not realizing what is happening.

Jonah says, "Well, maybe I am not the peaceable kind of fighter. Preacher Brent says, Oh, aww." Jonah hears his father's voice becoming weak and turns quickly and runs up to his father and responds, "Pa! Pa! I'm sorry, Pa! I didn't mean it. I'm an outlander, Pa. Please, oh my God, please." His father hugs him as Jonah cries in the preacher's arms.

Preacher Brent says "You got to make it right boy. Make it right with God, yea hear." Jonah responds, "I will! I will Pa. Pa!" Jonah holds on tight as the preacher rocks him in his arms, a flood of tears streams down Jonah's face.

Abruptly, Joshua opens the door as he hears all the commotion with his father and discovers Jonah has caused the preacher's attack. Joshua responds, "What are you doing here? You know his heart is bad." Joshua pushes Jonah away from his father and begins caring for the preacher. Jonah replies, "I want to come home. I told Pa." Joshua responds, "Go get the bottle over there. It helps him with his heart." J

onah goes and gets the bottle from the house that is sitting on a table and runs out and gives it to Joshua. Jonah says, "So is he going to be all right?" Joshua says, "Yeah, he's gonna be just fine." Jonah looks at him with a look of guilt and shame and starts heading toward his horse. Joshua yells out, "Where you going? Jonah! Jonah!" Jonah leaps on his horse and begins to ride away like lightening toward town.

As Jonah enters the town, he sees Larcey heading toward the saloon and they both enter together. Jonah sees May standing by an active card looking on as the player deals the hands to the cowhands. May looks up at Jonah with a surprise on her face and responds, "Well, looky here, there you are. You mean to keep a girl waiting forever for you?"

185

Jonah looks at May strangely with a hurtful broken stare. May replies, "You alright honey? You look like something's wrong." Larcey is at the bar drinking in the background and having a conversation with the bartender. Jonah says, "I almost killed my father."May's get a stone-gray look of shock on her face. "What! What happened?" Jonah moves her away from the card game toward a corner near the bar.

Jonah responds, "We were talking, and I got him all riled up. He has a bad heart. He had an attack." May hugs him tight and holds him close and looks him in his eyes. "Oh, honey I'm sorry." A moment later, Larcey walks over drunk from having one too many and grabs May by the bottom and Jonah gets enraged. Jonah shouts," Leave her alone!" Larcey is tussling with May as she pulls away from his unwanted attention.

Larcey says, "You can't keep her all to yourself now. You know May's a working woman." Larcey whispers something in May's ear and she slaps him across the face. He laughs and says, "Isn't that right May." He hits her across the butt again as she is trying to walk away. Jonah says, "I'm not going to tell you again!"Larcey grabs her wrist as she is walking away.

May pulls away from him. "Let me go!" Larcey now has a tight grip on May's wrist and appears to be hurting her as she struggles to get free from him.Larcey says, "Don't act like you better than me. Look at what you do here. You no better than me!" Larcey slaps May across the face and she falls to the floor. Jonah turns around and punches Larcey in the face and knocks him down hard to the floor. Everyone in the saloon stops and looks at Larcey as he gets up from the floor.

In shame, Larcey runs out of the saloon and gets on his horse and rides off toward home. Jonah goes over and helps May get up. "You alright?" May says, "I'll be okay." Jonah embraces her and soothes her and then makes her sit down to gather herself. He then gets up and tells May, "I got to go, I got some things to work out. You going to be alright? May looks up at him with an assuring face, "Yes. Go on. I'll be fine."

McCray and his cowhands are working the ranch clearing some wooded land. They are dragging broken tree branches and piling them to be burned. Mike looks over at Larcey with curiosity and asks Larcey, "Where is Jonah?" Larcey abruptly answers. "I don't know, Pa. He left the saloon last night and I haven't seen him since."

Mike steps closer and looks Larcey in the eye. "What do you mean? What happened to make him leave? He came by here last night and told me about how you got those outlanders!" Larcey has a bruise on his face and is thinking about the embarrassment Jonah caused in the saloon last night. He doesn't really care where Jonah is and really wants him to stay away. He begins telling Mike lies to make Jonah look bad in his eyes.

"Yeah, we got them, but Pa, Jonah's been acting strange." Mike laughs and dismisses what Larcey tells him. "Jonah always acts strange." Larcey is now irritated and tries again to convince Mike to distrust Jonah. Larcey replies, "I mean he's been acting differently, kind of strange. You know stranger than usual." Mike moves away from his son with disdain and shouts. "I don't care what you think! You find my boy Jonah and bring him back here."

Larcey throws down the branches he is pulling to the pile and shouts. "Your boy Jonah?" He touches his chest. "I'm your boy, Pa. Jonah ain't your son." Mike puts his hand on Larcey shoulder trying to soothe him and looks directly at Larcey. "He's a better son than you are. When I send him out to do things, he gets em done."

Larcey's face is completely red with astonishment that his father feels closer to Jonah than him. "What are you saying? You're not putting Jonah before me, are ya, Pa?" Mike puts his chest out with pride and states, "I plan to leave half this ranch to Jonah when I die." Larcey walks up fast on his father and gets in his face and shouts, "This ranch is a McCray Ranch and that's what it's gonna stay!"

Mike says, "No need to worry son, I'm sure Jonah will share the ranch with you." Mike reaches out to touch Larcey on the shoulder again and Larcey pushes him away. Larcey gets a look of realization on his face that his father doesn't care about him or his mother. Larcey says, "Ma, is right. Jonah looks just like Ms. Elizabeth, that's why you are doing all this." Mike begins to get angry and moves close to Larcey and tells him, "You watch your mouth boy."

Larcey is deeply hurt; tears are on the brim of his eyes as he makes one last plea to his father. Larcey says, "Why can't you just be happy with me the way I am?" Mike looks at his son in disappointment. "I do love you boy, I just." He goes to touch Larcey and Larcey jerks himself away.

Larcey puts his hand up in rage and balls his fist, as if he is going to hit his father then pulls it back. "Don't say anything else. I know what I have to do." Mike moves really close to his son's face in a seedy sly way. "What are you going to do? You don't have it in you, boy. You just don't have the guts." Larcey darts his eyes toward his father and snatches away from him. "I'm going, and when I see Jonah, I'm going to kill him!" Mike shouts, "You go get Jonah! Ben you go with him."

Mike looks at Larcey with a dirty smile and says, "You won't kill Jonah. He might kill you. Be careful, boy. When a man has that much hate in him, he can do "pritt" near anything." Larcey runs over to the corral and grabs a hunk of the horse's mane as he leaps on top of the saddle. Larcey looks over at Ben and shouts, "Let's ride!" Ben smacks his horse and shouts, "Ha!"

Jonah is riding up to his father's house and goes inside and walks up to his father's room. The preacher is sound asleep and resting peacefully. Jonah just stands over him looking at him realizing he almost lost him too. A rush of emotion comes over Jonah as he hurries down the steps and mounts his horse and leaves.

As he is riding, he sees the Barnaby family working to rebuild their barn that he and the McCray men burned and destroyed. Jonah rides up to where they are gathering wood and asks, "Need any help?" Bills turns and looks at him realizing Jonah is trying to apologize.

Bill says, "We can always use help." Alice comes over with a caring look on her face and says, "I been praying for you to come back home." Jonah bows his head in shame as Alice embraces him. Jonah says, "Yes, the prodigal son has finally returned home."

REDEMPTION

Matt walks up on Jonah fast and Jonah steps back for fear Matt will strike him. Matt gives Jonah a burnt piece of wood. "Good to see you. Can you hold this up since you burned it up?" Jonah takes off his hat and bows his head in submission and looks up at Matt. "I, I am sorry for that Matt. I going to make it up to you." Matt with a look of disbelief blurts out a question. "Jonah? Why are you here?"

Bill puts his hand up motioning Matt to stop badgering Jonah. "Matt! It doesn't matter why he is here. Can't you see he's different?"Alice touches Jonah's back and tries to assure him that they have forgiven him. "Yes, you are different, Jonah. Why don't you tell us what has happened to you to change you so?" Jonah wrings his hat in his hands and get a tragic look on his face. "Pa almost died last night."

Bill gets a look of terror on his face and grabs his chest. " What! Oh no! I'm sorry, Jonah." Alice says, "Me too. But you haven't been out there much to see him over these many months. Why did you go out there last night?" Jonah gets a blank stare on his face. "I don't know. I thought a lot about what happened to my Pa.

And how my Ma would not be happy with what I have become." Matt looks at Jonah with disdain and says abruptly, "What do you mean? You didn't seem to care much before." Jonah shouts and his voice cracks. He begins to break down and cry as he is speaking. "I do care, I mean, but… well, everything seemed to keep reminding me of that night. The night when McCray's men dragged my Pa and left him for dead. Then all of you were standing around doing nothing."

Matt is not moved by Jonah's tears and keeps pushing at Jonah walking up on him in frustration. "You almost lost him before, and you left home without a care or concern." Alice sees Jonah is hurting and seeking forgiveness. Alice shouts, "Matt, watch what you say!" Jonah wipes his eyes and realizes he has damaged so much of the lives of the people he loves.

He understands why Matt is angry. Jonah says, "No, it's all right. Matt's right. But I realized last night that I couldn't bear losing Pa. It was at that moment that I realized I had to go home." Matt throws his hands up in the air and walks toward the barn and shouts, "It's about time!" Alice shouts, "Matt!" Jonah gets a solemn look and says, "No, it's alright. He has a right to how he feels."

Alice gives Matt a disapproving look of warning as she tells Jonah, "Go on Jonah." Jonah says, "Well, I realized I had nothing. I knew it then. All my money, everything I had come from the McCray's. It's like eating with pigs." Matt realizes that Jonah is sincere and begins to reassure him by talking about a teaching of Preacher Brent. "That's what Preacher Brent taught us. To be peaceable.

Vengeance is mine sayeth the Lord." Jonah looks at Matt with a tired face. "Don't preach to me, Matt. My Pa preached to me all last evening and my heart is full right now." Matt looks at Jonah in earnest and asks, "What did he say?" Jonah walks over to Matt as he feels he has forgiven him now and tells him. "He taught me how it's more important to do what God wants you to do than what you want to do.

He said a man must make up his mind about what he believes in. He said you're more of a coward when you fight than when you find ways not to fight, and work things out." Bill pats Jonah on the back. "That's good, Jonah. You seemed like you listened this time." Jonah feels more assured now and has a look of peace on his face.

195

"I did, I really did. My Pa said I must make it right with God. I am still learning that part, but I am willing to try now. That's why I'm here now to make amend. I know it will take time to earn your trust again. But I am truly sorry for the trouble I caused. "They all hug Jonah and make him feel the love that he needs so much. Bill says, "We forgive you, Jonah. What are you going to do about Old man McCray?" Jonah gets a strange look on his face and throws his hand up. "Nothing. He doesn't control me. I am my own man."

Bill looks concerned because he knows that McCray is a vengeful man and may come after Jonah to harm him. Bill says, "Jonah, you know you been working for McCray for a long time." Jonah responds, "I know I have." Bill puts his hand on Jonah's shoulder and looks him in the eyes with deep worry and tells him. "Do you think he is going to let you go? He thinks of you as his son." Jonah shouts, "I only have one Pa, and no one can replace him."

Alice has a look of distress and asks, "What are you going do?" Jonah says, "Don't worry about me. I will be fine." Jonah gets on his horse and begins to ride away.

He looks back and waves at them as he rides off. Bill runs up behind Jonah and shouts, Jonah, "Wait let all of us go with you." Jonah keeps riding and shouts back, "No, this is something I must do by myself. No, I mean trusting in God." Matt has a proud look on his face, and he says," I will pray for you, Jonah. I believe God will provide." Jonah replies, "Me too Matt. Me too."

Jonah speeds his horse up and gets into a full gallop as he hurries toward town. When Jonah arrives in town, May runs out of the saloon with an uneasy look on her face. May says, "Jonah, where have you been? Larcey McCray is looking for you. Jonah, Larcey is acting crazy, talking about killing you." Jonah gets a look of alarm. "Killing me. Why would he want to kill me?" May says, "Because he believes that you are going to steal his ranch. His father told him that he was leaving half of everything to you."

Jonah's voice heightens as he tells May, "What! I don't want his ranch. I don't want anything from him." May replies, "Jonah, Larcey is riding up. Be careful. "Jonah turns and gives May his gun and she gets a confused look. Jonah looks over and sees Larcey heading past the general store and the townsfolk notice that a gunfight is about to start.

The townsfolk all start moving inside and the sound of windows and doors closing can be heard all around. Jonah walks up the town street as Larcey is getting down off his horse. Jonah doesn't have his gun anymore, but he continues walking toward Larcey. Larcey walks up and forms a stance with his hand on his gun holster. He yells out, "Where have you been, Jonah?" Jonah shouts back with confidence, "Since when do I answer to you?"

Larcey's face shows anger as he says, "Since my father went crazy and said he was going to leave you *our* land." Jonah shouts back to Larcey. "I don't want your land or anything you have." Townspeople are all looking through doors and windows and Jonah and Larcey are preparing to have a gunfight. Larcey moves over as if he is going to make a move for his gun.

Then he notices that Jonah has no gun in his holster. Hot with anger, he doesn't think but continues to talk. Larcey replies, "Why? Why don't you want it, Jonah? My father loves you more than me. He told me so." Jonah knows Larcey is hurting and tries to soothe him. "No, he doesn't! You have to stand up to him and help him understand how wrong that is."

Larcey hits his gun holder nervously as he steps closer to Jonah. Larcey responds, "I can't do that! But if I kill you, it will prove to him that I am worthy to be his son and not you." Jonah with apprehension tells Larcey killing him is not the answer. Jonah says, "If you kill me, you will only make him love me more." Larcey looks confused as he is trying to figure out what to do. "What are you talking about? If I don't kill you, people will think I'm a coward."

Jonah says with confidence, "No, they will think you are if you do." Jonah motions to his holster and shows Larcey that he doesn't have a gun. Jonah says, "I don't have a gun anymore and I am turning my back. Are you going to shoot me in the back, Larcey?" Jonah turns his back to Larcey and begins to walk away. He shouts, "Then shoot!"

Larcey is now anxious and frustrated with Jonah, Larcey yells, "You turn around! Turn around and face me like a man." Jonah keeps walking toward the saloon and shouts back. "I'm not going to fight you, Larcey. I don't have to." Angry and troubled by Jonah's response, Larcey rips his gun out and points it at Jonah, then quickly shoots it in the air.

In frustration, he yells, "Jonah, don't you walk away from me! Jonah, what will I tell Pa?" Jonah keeps walking and turns with confidence, looking Larcey in the eye. He shouts, "Tell him I'm an outlander! Tell him! He'll understand." Jonah gets near the saloon and May sees him, and in her excitement, she rushes into Jonah's arms almost knocking him over. Larcey's face is filled with distress as he beats his hand against his holster.

He turns and walks toward his horse and climbs on as he looks back at Jonah before he rides off. A worn-down farm shows age with a splintered wood porch and cracked windows. Preacher Brent is once again sitting in his wheelchair and the congregation are all standing around as he is preaching from the porch. A rustling is heard in the trees as Jonah rides up and throws the strap of his horse around a branch and walks over.

Preacher Brent says, "The Lord loves us, and he keeps us from harm. "Jonah makes his way through the church members and shouts out, "Yes, he does! Preach it preacher!" A light of happiness fills Preacher Brents' face as he is surprised by Jonah's entrance. The preacher touches Joshua and gives him his Bible as he looks long at Jonah.

Preacher Brent claps his hands in joy. "Let us celebrate and thank heaven for my son who was lost has returned home." Jonah looks at all the happy faces of the congregation. "Yes, Pa the prodigal son returns." In his excitement, Preacher Brent motions with his hand to Sister Barnaby to come over. "Sister Barnaby, let's prepare a big feast. Yes, and enjoy the blessing of the Lord!"

Joshua looks at his father and can't believe he just accepts Jonah back so easily. Joshua's face has a sad and disappointed look. "Pa, what are you doing after all Jonah has done? You take him back just like that! I have been here with you all these years not Jonah. I have taken care of you!" Preacher Brent grabs Joshua's hand and looks at him with loving eyes.

"Joshua, it's true you have been here all along, son. But, son, the Lord's words have been with you these many years. Your brother has been dead to all that we believe for so long. Now he has life in him again. You have to be happy for him. Right son?" Joshua's face changes to a calm and happy look. "Yes, Pa, yes I understand."

Preacher Brent says, "Let us praise God for his return!" All the people in the church begin to sing '*Bringing in The Sheaves*'. As Jonah looks over toward the trees, he sees May leaving a carriage and coming into the service. Jonah walks over and grabs her hand and leads her back to stand with him.

Larcey rides up to the McCray ranch slow with a fretful look on his face. As he approaches, Mike is sitting on the porch. He comes quickly over to speak to Larcey. He says, "Did you do it?" Larcey starts walking his horse into the barn. Mike McCray yells out to him. "Did you do it? Did you kill him?" Larcey comes out of the barn and walks up the steps where Mike is sitting on the porch and goes by him.

As he is passing, Mike grabs Larcey arm too tight. Mike says, "Answer me boy!" Larcey turns and looks at his father with despair and replies, "His God is bigger than my gun." He walks into the house as the door slams behind him. McCray sits on the porch with a perplexed look on his face.

Made in the USA
Middletown, DE
12 August 2022